Tales of the Hauraki Gulf

Short fiction and poetry

Auckland Writers

ISBN 978-1-0670340-5-4 (Paperback)
Front cover photography: Sue Glamuzina
Back cover photography: Melissa Gunn
Cover design, interior design and formatting: Melissa Gunn

Contents

Foreword

It's been an honour to put together this anthology of work, celebrating Tīkapa Moana - the Hauraki Gulf. This work, like the Gulf, is incredibly diverse, featuring both emerging and established writers, aged 6-90.

When I originally put the idea forward to some Auckland writers to do an anthology, I had no idea that we would go on to make a trilogy, have one hundred collaborators, nine of whom have contributed to all three books, and give so many first time writers the chance to feature alongside renowned writers and artists.

Personally, I need the ocean like I need vegetables. I have spent a lot of my life around the Hauraki Gulf - I learnt to drive a launch there, watched my son catch a hammerhead shark (by mistake) and had another son float away in a dinghy after a 'you won't believe where a wasp stung me' story and I had to swim after him, getting him back to safety an hour later. I even lost the diamond from my engagement ring somewhere on the beach at Motuihe Island and celebrated my 20th wedding anniversary with a ferry trip to Waiheke Island. This is my connection to the Gulf, and I know that the other contributors have their own special bond and unique memories of the Gulf... Perhaps you do, too.

Please enjoy reading this collection of stories, articles and poems, and then maybe head to the beach for fish and chips with an L&P.

Sue Glamuzina

The Gulf from Above

Andrew Holdaway

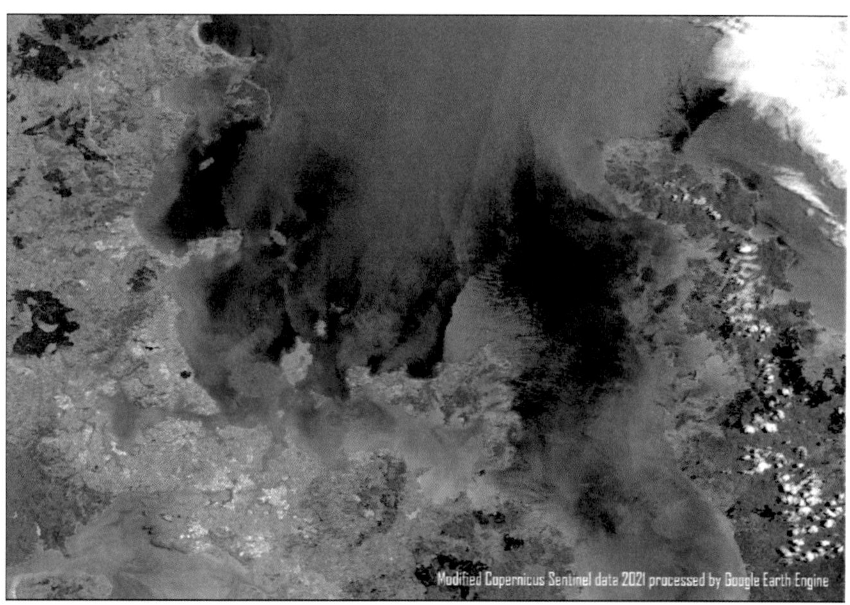

True colour image of the Auckland Gulf, captured on Christmas day, 2021. Visible is Auckland City, and the many islands of the Gulf, including Rangitoto, Motutapu and Waiheke, surrounding the turquoise water of the Tāmaki Strait.

Hauraki

Matthew Chamberlain

All the rocks have names, and I know none of them. I cry out to them anyway. Perhaps they will take pity on a shipwrecked soul. Though you need a ship to be shipwrecked, and mine is beneath the surf along with all who sailed on her. Save me, solitary me, clinging to this splintered spar. The rock. That took us down should be cursed, whatever name it goes by.

I yell at the wind too, and it pays no heed. It comes from the north, I think, though I cannot tell in this place. All the directions are turned about. I suppose this wind has a name too? Should I bother to learn it in what time I have left, short as it may be? Will it teach me? I am no sailor; I have no knowledge of the deepness that carries me. But I know I am tired and alone, and no one answers my calls.

No sailor, nor mechanic either, despite what I said at the Company's Offices. Free passage was granted with a swift stamp of papers, no further questions asked. I thanked the clerk and left immediately, lest I gave either of us a chance to reconsider. The ship sailed three days later for the far-flung colony with me and my meagre possessions aboard.

The filthy fog of London faded from view, and I examined my heart. Hope was not found, for I had left it at the house next to my father's cold form and his endless debts. Rather, relief assumed its place, shouldering guilt aside, and filling up my thoughts.

Now I damn my former self. *A fool to leave and a fool to come.* Better to stay and live a pauper's life than risk this end. Months of travel and I have only seen this new land from the deck. A deck that threw me off as we foundered. I don't even know which way to swim for shore. The stars make strange shapes I cannot navigate. I should not be here, screaming into the night, soaked, and colder than I have ever been.

My father would have called this a test. "Providence comes to those who persevere." He would have known. He kept going when all things told him to stop, even when the consumption took him to bed for the last time. Thinking about him sends huge shivers down my arms and legs. It seems nothing to do with the cold.

My personal faith comes to me as the last car on a too-long train. I remember that cavernous church, the preacher's words, those splinter-filled pews. What was the prayer? Will it save me now? I struggle for the words, getting them wrong, and then anger bursts out of me. "Is this my lot then? Am I punished? Forsaken?" I cannot change my grip on the wet wood to shake a fist, so I strike at the heavens with each word, aiming at a God I had forgotten to believe in.

I babble. Time slips around me with the waves. I am thirsty and cannot drink. I mumble the name of God and ask Him to save me. My clothes tug with heavy folds and ask me to sleep. I doze and drift.

Sobbing wakes me. A mournful moaning all around. I think it is gulls. I squint, afraid they will take my eyes like the ravens I left behind. Through the salt on my lashes, I see the dawn sun. Its red arms paint the sky while catching my breath and turning it silver. A lethargic shudder passes through me. There are no birds, but the moaning continues, louder, and then I see her.

Out of the blood-coloured sky, she comes. Her feet skip the whitecaps. A cloak of dark feathers gathers around her body like furled wings. In flickering light, she approaches, and my eyelids fly apart. I suddenly see I am surrounded by islands like dark green whales breaching the surface. They pull toward me. The sea bucks, raising me high. The moaning peaks as she arrives and then silence falls as her mouth opens.

Golden lines cover her chin, rippling as she speaks. Her voice is distant dripping in a dark cave, a hurricane through the wood, the centre of the flame. "I have come."

The language is not the King's, yet I understand it. Not by my ears, but in my chest. I try to answer. A croak escapes my lips, shorn of words. I think instead, and pray she understands. *Save me. Please.*

"The time for saving has passed." She sounds like my mother, impossible as that is, and I fear I understand her too well.

Do I know her? Who is she that walks on water and speaks with the voice of the woman who died birthing me? This is not the God I prayed to. Is He even in this land? The preacher told me He was everywhere. But this is not His face. He does not have these eyes that swell and glow as they watch me. There is no cross here, no stained glass. What manner of Goddess has come to me then?

The wind picks up at this thought, and its cold fingers drag across my face as if to force me south. The gusts move the cloaked woman's hair, and she flicks her hand. The wind leaves her but remains on me as if mollified. It no longer feels cold, and I wonder if she knows its name.

She smiles at me like the first star in all Creation. "I know every name, including yours."

I try to croak again. There is no strength in me for it. I cannot remember the last time I took a breath and find I have no fear left, even of this awesome Goddess. She grows in my vision, blocking out the sky, her gaze enormous. *Teach me. Please.*

Her cloak opens and the moaning voices wail anew in a mighty choir. Red light envelopes my mind, warm as the hearth, warm forever.

My body slips off the broken spar. The ocean sighs down and away, the islands return to their places, and the north wind scurries across the breakers. For a short while it hunts, then it gives up in a flurry, seeing its prey has gone where it cannot follow.

From the arms of the Goddess, I farewell it by name.

Breakers. Image: Susan Glamuzina

Shearwater

Brittany Mathias

Flesh-footed shearwater near Aotea/Great Barrier Island

Great Barrier - Visiting a Friend

Jenny Clay

flying in
over the gulf

kākā in the peach trees
take pecks
with large beaks
and let the peaches drop

a family of rabbits
bounce in and out of burrows
in the field opposite

Viv has large
and small
metal sculptures
in the shed

succulents by the door
a view of Little Barrier
across the sea

kept separate
in seclusion
for protection

at night
dark sky
stars penetrate

Dreaming of the Winds

Melissa Gunn

Hauturu-o-toi/Little Barrier Island. Acrylic on canvas.

Learning to Live Together

Brittany Mathias and Shaun Lee

Kekeno/fur seals make a comeback to the shores of the Hauraki Gulf/Tīkapa Moana/Te Moananui-ā-Toi

How would you react to finding a leopard seal lazing on your local marina pier or a seal pup out for a day on the town at the local KFC?

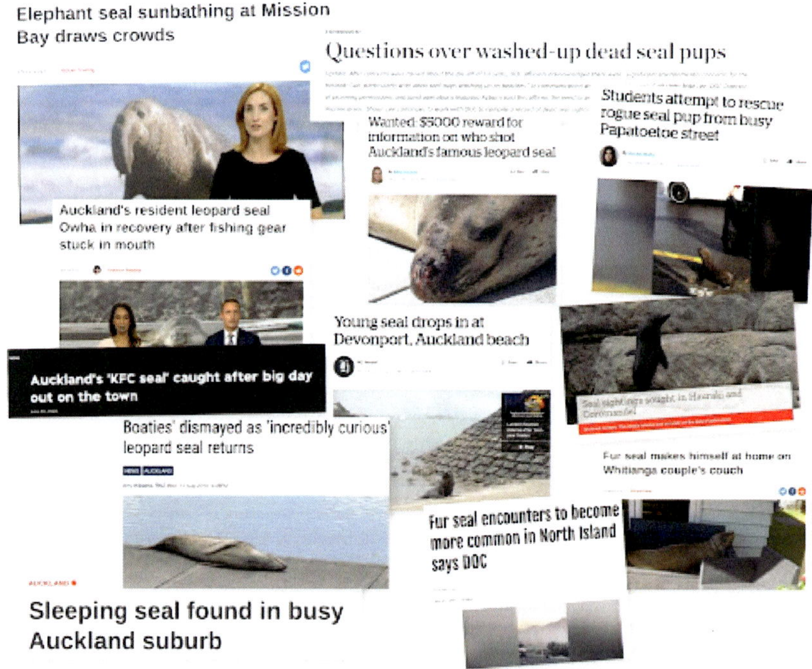

Seals are making headlines as they return to the shores of the Gulf

Despite the declining health of the Gulf, seals are making a comeback. After being hunted to near extinction for over a century, these marine mammals are returning. And while it's a conservation success story, interactions with humans are becoming increasingly more common.

When humans and animals interact it often leads to conflict. This can have devastating impacts for both species. Wild animals can behave unpredictably when put under stress and may defend themselves if they feel threatened causing injury or even death to humans. In some parts of the world, tourists approaching wildlife too closely has prompted officials to euthanise individuals in order to protect public safety. For example, in 2022, "Freya", a walrus in Norway was euthanised due to fears of potential harm to humans and inability to maintain animal welfare. Despite dozens of pleas from officials to give her space, curious onlookers continued to approach her to take photos, throw objects at her, swim with her and surround her in large numbers.

Over time animals may become accustomed to humans and may seek out human contact. Conditioned seals can become a problem as they may seek to 'play' with beach goers and swimmers. And then sometimes, well-meaning people think an animal needs assistance, when they are actually doing more harm than good. For example, beachgoers will often try to feed seals, thinking they are sick or injured. Human food is unhealthy for wildlife, and regular access to it can cause seals to become reliant on us for their meals, causing them to no longer seek out natural food sources. People have even been recorded trying to return seals to the water thinking that the animals are stranded. For example, someone once removed a young pup from a beach on the South Island and took it on the ferry to be assessed by a vet in the North Island. Unfortunately, the seal was too young to survive without its mother and had to be put down.

Of course, not all interactions with wildlife are negative.

Interactions with wildlife can improve human wellbeing and lead to increased support for wildlife conservation. As the human population expands, we continuously adapt our behaviour to live harmoniously with one another and protect wildlife. These adjustments are an ongoing effort as we learn about each other, and what's working.

Seals and sea lions in New Zealand

When the first Polynesians arrived in New Zealand around 800 years ago, our shores would have looked very different – fur seals and sea lions would have been found throughout the coastal area. Māori would have hunted them in big numbers – living in large colonies, seals were easy to find, providing a good source for food and clothing.

As Europeans arrived in the late 18th century, sealers and whalers came in the hundreds, hoping to make their fortune – catching seals for food, fur and oil. Soon seal skin hats, coats and footwear were being sold throughout Britain. Seal blubber was rendered to provide oil for lamps. Sealing would continue until 1946, decimating our seal populations to near extinction.

Seals and sea lions belong to a group of mammals known as the pinnipeds, which have limbs that are modified into flippers and streamlined bodies for efficient movement through the water. Four species of seals are regularly seen around the New Zealand coastline.

The seals of Aotearoa New Zealand. Image: Shaun Lee & Brittany Matthias

Kekeno/New Zealand fur seals

Kekeno are the most common marine mammal on our shores, found throughout our coastline as well as Western and Southern Australia. The last population estimate was in 2001 which put the population at 200,000 individuals (it's higher now, but by how much is unknown) - probably 5 to 10% of the number before humans arrived. Breeding colonies occur as far north as Moutohorā Island, off Whakatāne. However, there is no known breeding colony within the Gulf.

Fur seals in New Zealand follow a predictable seasonal pattern, with newly weaned yearlings dispersing from the breeding colonies from May to September. Juvenile fur seals have been found over 1,000 km away from their place of birth. Tagged fur seals from Cape Foulwind on the West Coast have been recorded in the Gulf. As the newly weaned juveniles begin to explore the world (a bit like a teenager on their OE) we start to see an influx of seals on our shores, often putting them in conflict with people and dogs. There is an ongoing effort to find out why so many Kekeno are found dead on the beaches of the Gulf. Regular mortality events for Kekeno in early September are dominated by pups and yearlings. More than half of them do not appear to be dying of starvation.

Although seals are marine mammals, they spend a lot of time on land—coming ashore to rest, moult and breed. On land seals have been found in unusual places such as backyards, drains and roads. They can travel quite far inland, often by following rivers or streams. The Department of Conservation (DOC) receives a huge number of calls every year from concerned members of the public who are worried that these animals are sick or injured. Sneezing, coughing and regurgitating are normal seal behaviour and shouldn't be mistaken as a sign of distress.

DOC uses a hands off approach when it comes to wildlife and will only intervene if an animal is in immediate danger such as getting too close to a road, entangled in fisheries debris, being harassed by people/dogs or seriously injured. If we can educate ourselves on the natural behaviours of these animals then we are better placed to help seals when they really are in trouble.

Steps forward:

Managing human wildlife conflict requires management of both animals and people. This requires input from not only scientists and conservation managers but local communities as well.

Here are some ways we can help through policy and legislation, community outreach and awareness, and through our individual outcomes.

- To reduce conflict, safe places for seals should be planned for in regional coastal management plans.

- Seals are part of an intact ecosystem; fishing methods and seal prey biomass should be considered in the Hauraki Gulf Fisheries Management Plan.

- Citizen science is an important tool for understanding how our seal populations are recovering and learning about how seals are using the Gulf. Citizen science promotes collaboration between conservation managers, researchers and members of the public. Sightings of seals can be reported on iNaturalist.nz

- Local communities around the Gulf need to take ownership of their backyard and be kaitiaki/guardians of the places they visit. This could mean educating yourself on how to watch wildlife responsibly, learning more about the Gulf's seals, keeping your dogs on a leash when out for a walk or picking up rubbish at your local beach.

If you encounter a seal while enjoying the Gulf enjoy the experience – remember how lucky we are to live alongside these beautiful animals.

Orapiu

Elizabeth Morton

I break apart, little place. I break apart in the septic fug of you,

oranged water spilling from the faucet, the bleached hills.

I have refused each way out. The thousand desolations of seeing

the moon, same moon of my childhood, of my father's father's
loneliness.

Little place, my brother is hiding in the out-house. I have scared
him

into corners, even here. Evening, we will walk the paper road

to the ridgeline, peel back bracken and gorse flower, study our lives

for scraps of our birth-stories. Our silly torches scaling the trunks

for possums, making myth of the black and white holt.

Mānuka bent forward like ghosts, the hooved scoria, a bulldozer

parked up on a bank. I break apart in the salt-scape, little place.

Evening, and the Pollocked shit of fairy terns burns white on the jetty.

Starboard green of a yacht. Mackerel flashing their metal anatomies,

sluiced and slippery. You knew I would fall for it –

Childhood studying me from the blackened beach, a stranger.

Have you been here before? a nine-year-old might say, and I will say

In a dream, like this is not my moon, my gorse flower, my ghost bay.

Evening. Image: Susan Glamuzina

Rangitoto

Sue Russell

Rangitoto Island. Acrylic on canvas.

Rangitoto earrings. Sue Russell.

Three Times the Charm

Kynan Wright

Shelly eased the boat off the dock with a slow exhale. Her shoulders loosened as she savoured a rare moment of silence and freedom. Sure, there was the deep thrum of the motor, the lapping of the waves, and indistinct noises from a waking Viaduct, but *he* was quiet. That's all that mattered.

She had expected to feel jumpy as she approached Wynyard Crossing, but Shelly steered with sure hands. The bridge raised smoothly, and she waved cheerily at the operator's booth. The morning sun set the glass aflame, making it impossible to tell if they were waving back.

Today was the first day that Shelly had helmed the *Lucky Star*. Rain or shine, sober or drunk, Jack had insisted on steering. Any other suggestion would elicit rants about the dangers of female drivers, or on his worst days, a raised fist.

This morning, he was unusually quiet. Jack sat rigidly on the passenger seat, eyes hidden behind sunglasses and with his mouth closed. He could pass for dead if not for the muffled snoring. Shelly darted glances at him, fearing he would wake and shatter the dream.

The *Lucky Star* inched out of the Viaduct Basin, but couldn't properly stretch her legs until she was clear of the speed-restricted lanes. Still, leaving it was another tick on a mental checklist that had cautiously developed over years of suffering. Shelly wasn't naïve enough to start celebrating, but her spirits rose all the same.

Now clear of most of the traffic, Shelly set a course and double-checked her rucksack. She rummaged through the contents, rehearsing the plan in her head. Tying her hair back into a crisp ponytail, she approached Jack. She checked that he was securely fastened, that his cap and sunnies were in a natural position, and that he didn't seem likely to wake. Satisfied, Shelly opened up the throttle and headed towards Little Barrier Island.

She avoided the normal fishing spots, opting for a quieter area. Her heart thumped as she scanned the horizon, trying to confirm that they were alone, at least for a little while. A lone yacht came into view, crawling along the Gulf in the flaccid wind. Minutes felt like hours as it faded from view.

With the moment upon her, Shelly froze. Her mind spun with conflicting fears, while reasons and excuses grappled in the background.

"Nnnnngh."

"Oh God."

Jack started to move, slowly at first, but increasing in urgency as he realised that something was wrong. Shelly clutched her head in her hands, shaking as she repeated her plea to the almighty.

"Oh God. OH GOD!"

"Mngh-ph!"

Jack was discovering the difficulty of trying to talk through duct tape. The cable ties at his wrists and ankles strained as he tried to free himself, and Shelly instinctively took a step back, nearly tripping on her rucksack. It opened, revealing the billy club. She closed her eyes and went completely cold.

Breathe in. Breathe out. Just like you practised. Shelly opened her eyes and scooped up the billy club. She strode behind her struggling husband and took a comfortable stance. Her mind flashed back to happier times when he'd first shown her how to fish. He'd held a snapper aloft and struck it sharply with the club as she winced.

"Three times is the charm, then toss it into the chilly bin."

She struck the back of his head with all her might. Once. Twice. Three times. He stilled. She retrieved the pliers from her bag and freed him from his restraints. She dragged him to the back of the boat and shoved him with all her might. He tumbled into the water, disappearing into the depths. It was done.

Shelly waited a few minutes before calling the Coast Guard. She didn't have to fake tears when they arrived, and his passing was considered a tragic but preventable accident. Unfortunately for Jack, he steadfastly refused to wear a life-jacket and would brag about that fact to anyone who would listen.

Boating. Image: Susan Glamuzina

The Northwestern Motorway

J A Redmore

I wake to holiday-traffic clouds
steadily obeying the three-second rule
on day trips from Waitematā
to Manukau.

Each tick of the trees
kingfisher flurry
rumour from rosellas
resignation of leaf
press of my jandal on the estuary's cocktail pathway
whisper of lead on memory
exhale of belly breath,
resounds
like an off-peak Coromandel cove.

While the Northwestern motorway
ponders irrelevant prevalence.

Kingfisher

Sue Carpenter

Acrylic on canvas

Sentinel Beach

Susan Glamuzina

The harbour bridge hums
busy people rush
shops in the city make sales
accountants in offices crunch numbers
yet five minutes away
there's a quiet bay
where a retired couple lounge in the sun
young couple on a blanket read books in bliss
three boys take turns on a swing
lapping water
greets the sand
where in the shade
on a hammock
I breathe

Rangitoto from Takapuna Beach. Denise T O'Hagan

Just Another Race Day

Bruce Wyness

"Hi Wazza, looks like a good breeze out there, perfect sailing weather." I tossed my sailing bag into the cabin. I'd taken out the wet weather gear; wouldn't need that today, but kept the sunhat and lotion.

"It'll be a scorcher," said Den. "The forecast is a steady 15 knots from the southwest, veering further west later in the day. Depending on our course we could have a fast race with a couple of spinnaker legs."

It was my turn to supply the rum; I secured the bottle of Myers Dark in the locker. Al had brought Coke and ice, and Den a few beers in a chilly-bag, so we had all the essentials on board. I noticed that Wazza had washed the mugs, they'd needed it as they hadn't been cleaned for at least 2 months. Den and I checked to ensure the big red spinnaker and the new jib were stowed and all lines ready for use.

"Ready?" called Wazza. Den, Al and I gave him a thumbs up.

"OK, let's do it."

He started the tractor and towed the Elliot 7.4 on its trailer down the beach, turned and then backed through the surf until the yacht began to float off the trailer. Den pulled on the starter cord and got the outboard going. We cruised up and down the beach while Warren, the skipper, parked the trailer. The 10-minute flag went up on the Browns Bay clubhouse as Warren waded out through the waves and climbed onboard.

"Keel down, main up, jib up," he called, as he killed the outboard and swung it up out of the water. He didn't need to as we were already pulling on the halyards and setting the sheets. We'd sailed together for a few years so this was all easy.

"Course?" asked Al.

"Compass Dolphin return, so get the spinnaker set up, Den. We'll launch it as we cross the start line," said Wazza.

We went through the usual pre-race manoeuvres; a few tacking duels, trying to fool the other yachts into being at the wrong end of the start line, calling out dubious rule violations and generally having fun. The starting horn from the caravan on the beach (our clubhouse) blasted. The spinnaker was hoisted. It looked weird; I pulled on the sheet, but it just wouldn't set.

"I don't believe it," yelled Warren, slapping his forehead. "It's upside down!" The laughter, hooting and derogatory banter from the other yachts was loud and relentless. We cringed.

Den and Al scrambled to get the kite down, took the sheet off the head, placed it on the clew and recoupled the halyard.

Ready to hoist, again, skipper," said Al, then saluted and added, "Sir." He could be quite mocking sometimes.

Warren mumbled something we couldn't hear, then a bit louder, "Hoist the spinnaker."

Up she went and, fortunately, set immediately. We hadn't lost too much time and quickly took the lead back. We sailed away leading the fleet across the smooth water, heading south towards North Head. I was on the sheet controlling the set. It was an easy course as the wind was steady. A cold beer was thrust into my hand.

"Get that down before you faint from the heat." It was Al performing his duties as Sustenance Officer for the day. This was going to be a good race!

We sailed at around seven knots with an occasional burst to ten knots a few k's off the East Coast beaches for around ninety minutes.

Al had handed out some snack bars and another beer as we passed Campbells Bay. The crew took turns trimming the spinnaker while we slapped on sun lotion. The sky was blue, the sun blazing down and we were still leading the fleet by maybe 20 minutes.

The sound system was cranked up for a while and we sang along to Dire Straits and Pink Floyd; still making good progress. Probably got too relaxed because as we approached North Head the yacht yawed, and we saw we were heading straight for the No 6 channel marker buoy. A large leopard seal, maybe 2 metres long was perched on it. Wazza threw the tiller over but the yacht hit the buoy with a glancing blow. The seal reared up, lunged forward and landed on our foredeck where it studied us briefly then slid over the side. No one said a word, didn't need to really. We passed North Head and took the spinnaker down, raised the jib, tacked over and headed to Compass Dolphin near Mechanics Bay.

"OK, time for a rum," came the order from the skipper.

Al saluted "Aye, aye, Captain, Sir." So, the first rum of the day was poured and handed out. Tricky stuff really when keeping an eye out for other watercraft, trimming the big jib and trying not to spill any of the dark liquid. But we'd practised this over a few years and had almost perfected the art.

It was a busy day on the Waitematā with several other yacht races in progress, a large number of pleasure craft and fizz boats charging about, a cruise liner being escorted out by two tugboats and a few passenger ferries to keep clear of. We slipped into serious mode, drained the rum tot and concentrated on our course, calling out other craft near us to the skipper. We had the big jib up which restricted the forward view so Den, being the lightest, perched on the bow to keep watch and shout if any evasive action was needed. He must have been distracted as the skipper of one of the Waiheke Ferries came out onto his flying bridge when he thought we'd come too close to his vessel, and yelled something like,

"I weigh 280 tons, you are less than 1 ton so get out of my way."

We waved and tacked away but decided he was overreacting so tacked back. The wind took his parting words away.

The breeze had died a bit. It took us 30 minutes to get to Mechanics Bay, round the dolphin and set off to North Head again. Safely back across the harbour, another rum was ordered as we turned back towards the north. The wind had swung around so the jib was trimmed, the spinnaker bagged, then stowed below. We waved at a couple of the slower yachts in our race. They were still heading to the compass dolphin, and we were well in front and on time for a club record maybe.

As we sailed past Narrow Neck, Den pointed out towards Rangitoto Island and called out.

"There's a yacht out there with nobody on it." The sail was down, it was drifting. Our skipper changed course to sail towards it. As we approached, we spotted someone in the water in a life jacket, just bobbing around. Warren tacked, came about and sailed over. It was a little old man.

"Are you OK?" shouted our skipper. We all burst out laughing at the old man's reply "My name is Jack, I'm 83 years old and absolutely f....d."

I grabbed his jacket and we pulled him on board. He wouldn't have weighed more than sixty kilos and was shivering violently.

"Thanks, boys," he said. "I was ready to give up, been floating around here for an hour, I think".

We wrapped him in a blanket and gave him a double rum. He downed that and held his cup out for another.

"What happened, Jack?" I asked.

"Well, I sail out of Wakatere Yacht Club at Narrow Neck. Been doing this twice a week since me wife died ten years ago. Gets me out of the house, you see. I was having trouble with the rudder, so dropped the sail to get a better look at it. The boom slammed over, hit my shoulder and over I went. Bloody stupid really, thought my time had come and had been thinking it wasn't a bad way to leave really, floating around in the ocean."

His face became pale and his breathing shallow. I wondered if he was going into shock.

"Keep him talking," said Al.

"So, you live on the shore then, Jack?" asked Den.

Jack took a big breath and seemed to calm down. He chattered away about his three children, all boys. They keep in touch but they all lived overseas. He lived alone.

Den offered to sail Jack's yacht back to the beach and we sailed in close enough for me to help Jack off the Elliot, up the beach and into the clubhouse. There was a group of ladies chatting there, so I explained what had happened, handed his care over to them and started to leave, eager to get back to the race.

One of the ladies said, "C'mon Jack, get your trousers off, they are soaking wet and you're shivering."

Jack looked terrified and pleaded with me to stay and help him get undressed and changed. He didn't trust the yacht club ladies. So, I helped the 83-year old out of his trousers and underpants and into some baggy old sweatpants the ladies handed to me.

"Thanks, mate," said Jack.

I raced back down the beach, waded and swam to the yacht. We'd lost at least forty minutes and most of the fleet in our race had passed us.

"Hurry up!" yelled Al. "Were you waiting for a knighthood for rescuing him?" Al could be quite acerbic at times. I flipped him the universal hand sign for 'up yours' and climbed on board. We resumed the race, now behind most of the other boats.

The main was hauled up in record time.

"The wind has veered again, I might be able to fly the kite, let's get it up!" Wazza shouted. "We need to make up some time."

Den had already tied the spinnaker bag to the bow pulpit, the halyard was hooked up, and the brace and sheet lines run.

"Is it rigged right this time?" Den nodded.

"OK, send her up!" ordered the skipper. It was a perfect set, the sail filled quickly but then collapsed. We battled to keep it flying and had decided to take it down, but luck was with us and another wind shift brought the wind back astern for a perfect run up the coast. The yachts in front were using their genoas or jibs and we caught up on the slower boats. Jeers and wahoos echoed over the water as we sailed by. We were 4th across the finish line, twenty minutes after the first boat. With our nineteen-minute handicap that meant we were 39 minutes too late to win.

It was our lucky day though; the club handicapper gave us a 40-minute time allowance for the rescue so we ended up winning the race by one minute.

Back on dry land after retrieving the yacht and sorting out the gear, we rehashed the events of the day.

"Every race is different," mused Al. He often stated the bleeding obvious. We murmured agreement then celebrated our win and toasted spinnaker sets, the seal, the number 6 buoy, the ferry captain and Jack with a rum or three.

Sailing. Image: Susan Glamuzina

Waiomu Morning

Amanda Eason

Finding a moon chair behind the pantry door, I pad over the front lawn in bare feet and PJs to sit under the grandmother pōhutukawa for the view—a cuppa on the grass beside me. Her toes fix this cliff. Veins like wandering rivers bind her breadth.

A rope swing's slung over a shoulder and bands of red thread through her hair. Sounds overlap like waves at the bluff's base.

Goldacres. Image: Louise Pirret

First we must mention the road. There's nowhere else for it. Bottle-green mountains lean down at the last. Where quartz pebbles shuffle against the tide, gnawing the erupted flesh of Maui's fish—the

Thames Coast Road must run—a noose to land a feast.

Tucked between tar and tree, jewelled baches string out along the bays—decorating the Coromandel's throat: Kuranui, Thornton, Te Puru, Waiomu. Fishermens' fibrolite shanties, miners' cottages, 1920s mini-bungalows with barley-sugar and coconut-ice porch glass. From across the Firth, sun catches their windows—they glitter like prizes. I want one. We've paid mates' rates for this hillside Old Lady where miners staked claims starting with Pohue Stream at the back door—gold flecks shed to the sieve in 1873. Maybe tradesmen slithering under gappy floorboards even now are glittered when they stand, blinking—to shake dust from their trousers.

A December Saturday morning. Sporadic rumblings are four-wheel drives and clattering boats on trailers. Auckland decants to the peninsula—sprucing up boltholes for Christmas. Dented saucepans wash up in cupboards of chipboard and cupboards of rimu. Have ants been at the sugar? Have weevils webbed the Weetbix? Restocked shelves hold packets of gingernuts, candles, matches, dry pasta, coffee, tea, tins of baked beans. At least thumping the tank you know it's full. The weight of water the Ranges shouldered over winter! Rat droppings under the sink ... A winged scout swoops low. Are my purple-starred pyjamas pansies? She returns to sisters sipping syrup above. Tongues unroll as feathered feet sweep pollen into panniers.

Nightly, the ancestor draws water against the grain—replenishing nectaries for the morning's mass arrival. The thrumming hum I hear below all else—hundreds of hovering honey-bees harvesting. Later, I rescue one from the night toilet bowl, dipping in a piece of plastic to scoop her out—stepping through French doors to the dark deck—she's gone. The child can pee in peace and the summer night settles back about my shoulders like an old tartan travel rug—100% Pure New Zealand Wool.

Revenge of the Pā

Tremaine Ake

Generations guarded it.
Now they have been slain.
With this evil comes a renewed anger from the warm shores of Taranaki.
Now the Gods of fortune seek their payment from above their Kiwi Mount Olympus.
The Cosmos seeks to balance the world.
What you have taken must be given back.
No you may not see it.
But your children will feel the stake through the chest.
Your cursed treaty has blessed you with power, it was foretold it would only consume you.
Streams run dry, riverbanks explode, lakes turn septic.
Forests cut down in the name of the Queen.
The swamps drained, the mangroves uprooted, the green image continues.
The Queen is dead, the soldiers are dead, the settlers are dead.

The land lives on, it seeks to clean its back.
Soon it will shake the fleas off.
There's a meeting here tonight.
Soon the dawn of a new age will come.
Your stolen jewels will weigh you down in the water as you drown in the blood you cut from the throats of men, women and children.
Soon you will know the pain the guards felt.
But as your screams are filled by water, ash, fire and smoke you will still scheme.
So don't bother returning what you destroyed, you'll just take it back after another three years.
The guards no longer seek what they guarded.
Now they drown their sorrows in rye and pies.
The guards sit in land and sit in the bars singing the cosmos's revenge.

Escape from Motuihe Island

Bog Bakaric

Count Von Luckner held tightly to the German naval flag that Cadet Schmidt had neatly hand sewn from bedsheets. It was just on 6pm, 13th December 1917, the evening sky was clear, the trees on the hill above Waihaorangatahi Bay, Motuihe Island, swayed in the brisk northerly winds. The Count could not believe how his luck had turned for the better; despite his meticulous planning, and the lack of security on the island World War 1 internment camp, he needed things to be on his side.

Perched behind the beautiful old Pōhutakawa tree with its red flowers in full bloom, the Count gleefully glanced at the other nine men hiding behind him, then for a moment he looked with sadness at Lieutenant Colonel Charles Harcourt Turner, the commandant of the internment camp who had just disembarked from 'The Pearl'. He knew that on his escape, Mr Turner, as he had known him, would be in trouble with his superiors and no doubt be dismissed. The Count quickly pushed aside this train of thought. He was from a military family, in love with his motherland, his beloved Germany. This was war time, and New Zealand was the enemy.

The Count looked at The Pearl. It would be bad luck for Mr Turner, but it would be good luck for The Count, and an opportunity for him to pass on and rid himself of misfortune he had recently had.

Mr Turner had made the mistake of being relaxed with the

internees, befriending them, talking of his delight at his daughter joining him on the island for Christmas, and sharing the timing of her arrival. In contrast to Mr Turner's highly anticipated and well-planned arrival of his daughter with extravagant dinner plans, Count Luckner and his subordinates had plans of their own, to escape.

Mr Turner fussed over his daughter and beamed as he carried her luggage along the wharf up to his quarters. Count Luckner and the others interned in the camp had been particularly helpful and had put in a huge effort getting ready for the upcoming Christmas concert in the camp. Mr Turner couldn't wait to have his daughter enjoy the hot feast the internees had specially prepared for the visitor. He looked back at the Pearl and shrugged to himself. He always took the spark plugs out of the motor and they now jangled in his pocket. For once he would leave it tied up at the wharf, get his daughter settled in, have dinner, and moor the boat later in the evening.

As Mr Turner walked from the wharf and started up the hill, Count Luckner saw Freund, his trusted communications signalman. The ex telefunken employee followed close behind Mr Turner, then ducked into the bushes to disable the island's only telephone cable. The Count looked at his fob watch, before shouting in English from the top of the hill. That was accompanied by the faint smell of smoke. He smiled. It was smoke from a fire set to plan, by remaining internees at the camp to distract the forty guards on the island. First Officer Kircheiss did a shrill sharp wolf whistle, to which one of the cadets scurried down into the island's dinghy while all others, including Count Luckner, jumped onto The Pearl and got her started.

Count Luckner's first job on board was none other than to replace the boat's flag with the German flag. He had the supreme confidence to rely on his crew to do their respective tasks. The Pearl's engine roared to life, the cadet mechanics having replaced the spark plugs with spares they had secretly obtained, and pushed off the wharf. Count Luckner helped the cadet who had scuttled the dinghy on board and watched nervously as Freund, who, having done his task disabling the telephone line, sprinted along the wharf towards them.

The crew were now all watching intently as two uniformed guards came running down the hill and onto the wharf. Count Luckner could wait no longer for Freund, and barked an order to full power ahead. Freund, who was now nearing the end wharf at full sprint, had a panicked but determined expression on his face as the engine roared. The propellers turned furiously, chopping and churning the water at the stern. The boat was momentarily still, awaiting the due thrust forward.

Freund flung himself through the air off the wharf, desperate not to miss the escape. Count Luckner, a big man who towered over his crew, reacted quickly, reached out his large hands, just catching the slightly built Freund, as he thudded against the side of the launch, half-submerged in the water, then flung him effortlessly into the boat as it surged forward. The count tethered at the stern precariously before Cadet Mellert pulled on his shirt. Steadying him.

The Pearl had been bought, on behalf of at Lieutenant Colonel Turner's request, by the farmer on Motuihe from a Dr Endletsberger. It was a damaged boat, having been blown ashore in the big gales of early 1917. Repairs to the launch were carried out initially in Auckland and then on the island by the well-trained German Merchant Cadets from the North Germany Lloyd Shipping Line under the supervision of Lieutenant Colonel Turner.

The engine, though well-tuned and looked after by the cadets, barely pumped out 14HP. The launch itself was heavy from the added weight of the repairs that had made the launch seaworthy again. Count Luckner had had many discussions about whether eleven men and provisions on board were wise, compared to having the vessel lighter, faster and more nimble.

Count Luckner had stuck to his decision and ordered his men to take actions to slow down any subsequent chase after their escape, hence the scuttling of the island's only dinghy and cutting of the telephone line. The launch was not fast. It wasn't a planing vessel and as it passed between Motutapu and Motuihe Island, he ordered the crew to take the launch as close as possible to Motutapu Island. Carefully rolling up the German flag, he was nervous when he saw the Motuihe guards lined along the beach head. They hollered at him, cursing and swearing amid the crack of gunfire, as they tried to shoot at the launch, now well on the other side of the Motuihe Channel and close to the cliffs of Motutapu.

As they rounded the point to Home Bay, Motutapu, Count Luckner ordered the launch to be turned directly towards Matiatia Bay, Waiheke, near directly away from Home Bay. Looking back to Home Bay, he saw a soldier walking along the beach and waving casually. Count Luckner obligingly waved back, while noting the smoke rising from the large army tent camp site on Motutapu. He looked down into the launch and surveyed the pack of home-made grenades made from gunpowder and tins stolen from the Motuihe farmer's house, alongside the fake guns his crew had painstakingly made. He suddenly felt inadequately armed for the escape he had planned, particularly knowing the fire power available to those on Motutapu and possibly on other unknown outposts at the staging points of the Red Mercury Islands and the Kermadec Islands.

Von Zatorski brought the map he had hand-copied to the Count and First Officer Kircheiss, who pointed out towards Cape Colville at the tip of the Coromandel Peninsula, barking orders at the others emerging from within the Launch. Everyone was wide eyed, alert, tense. They all kept glancing back, half-expecting fast armed steamers to emerge from between Motutapu and Motuihe to pursue them, but they never came. Count Luckner was, however, already framed on their next destination, Cape Colville, and keen to get there early the next morning before turning down to Red Mercury Island.

The launch developed a drip leak from the starboard bow just after midnight, causing commotion on board, but it was well managed by the cadets who continued to prove their skill and resourcefulness. Count Luckner was on edge at that point. His mind reflected on the death of Douglas Page, the British sailor abroad the Horngarth. Count Luckner had captained the beloved SMS Seeadler, a 245 foot long ship that had captured or sunk 16 ships totalling 30,099 tonnes, in just 225 days, but his luck had changed when Douglas Page had died on the 10th March 1917.

An unexpected storm had pushed them significantly south as they rounded Cape Horn, not long afterwards, testing the seamanship of all on board the Seeadler. The ship had suddenly slowed after that, needing her hull to be cleaned. Some of the crew sick with scurvy, which meant she needed to stop. With the requirement to find safe haven, tend to the ship and restock it with supplies, Count Luckner had taken the SMS Seeadler to the Society Islands. However, while the ship was anchored outside the lagoon of the Mopelia Island, a Tsunami picked it up and wrecked it on the reef in August 1917.

Now, on The Pearl, Count Luckner laid down for a few hours below deck, but with the adrenaline flowing through him, all he could manage was rest with no deep sleep.

The next morning, two timber scows, the Moa and the Rangi which had anchored for a short period at Red Mercury Island, passed Mopelia Island. With great commotion, the crew of The Pearl caught up with the heavily-laden Moa. The Captain Jack Francis of the sister ship, Rangi, could only look on and make as much distance as possible from Count Luckner's raiders as they threatened ex-Navy Captain William Bourke and his crew with improvised grenades and fake guns.

Count Luckner ordered the timber cargo to be heaved overboard and set sail at once for the Kermadec Islands. Towing the Pearl, he looked back at the launch and the Hauraki Gulf, where he had only been a fleeting visitor, and feeling that his luck had returned, he was determined to keep The Pearl under tow with them so his luck should remain.

In the morning, having left the Hauraki Gulf, he awoke to the news The Pearl had been lost. Count Luckner looked back at the sea behind. Had his luck also been lost?

(Note: This is a historical fiction based on true events.)

Rangitoto. Image: Susan Glamuzina

Leopard Seals: A tale of resilience and wonder in the Hauraki Gulf

Tineke Joustra

The Hauraki Gulf, an expansive body of water surrounding Auckland, New Zealand, became the unexpected stage for a captivating tale that unfolded in 2015. Two leopard seals, a young male named Kohi and a female appropriately named "He owha nā ōku tupuna" (lovingly known as Owha), ventured into these waters around the same time, forever altering the narrative of these enigmatic creatures in New Zealand. Their arrival marked the beginning of a journey that would not only bring joy and fascination but also shed light on the misunderstood world of leopard seals.

Leopard seals, previously assumed to only be native to the frigid Antarctic waters, were believed to rarely travel North to more temperate climates. This made the presence of Kohi and Owha in the Hauraki Gulf around the same time a true rarity. Prior to 2015, knowledge about these marine mammals in New Zealand was limited, with only sporadic and historical sightings dotting the records. Little did anyone anticipate that the largest city in the country would become the backdrop for the unfolding story of these remarkable creatures.

The young male, Kohi, earned his name from the beach where he first made his appearance. His arrival was met with curiosity and excitement, marking the first chapter in the tale of leopard seals in the Hauraki Gulf as we knew it. The female Owha, named by the Ngāti Whātua Ōrakei with her full name "He owha nā ōku tupuna," meaning "treasured gift from our ancestors," added a cultural and spiritual dimension to the narrative. Owha's presence, in particular, would go on to leave an indelible mark on the region.

In the years following their arrival, Owha established herself as a resident of the Hauraki Gulf, making regular appearances at marinas and developing a familiarity with the local geography. From beaches to pontoons and jetski jetties, she seemed to feel at home, creating a unique bond with the community. However, the enchantment of Owha's presence was not solely confined to the recent past.

Photographic evidence emerged, revealing that leopard seals had been present in the Hauraki Gulf much earlier than previously thought. A sighting from Stanmore Bay in 1909 hinted at a historical connection between these marine mammals and New Zealand. Unfortunately, these encounters in the past were often marked by fear and a lack of understanding. Individuals like the one spotted in 1909 faced dire consequences, with many being shot or captured for zoos and Marineland attractions. In an era without the internet and comprehensive knowledge about these creatures, such actions were driven by a misguided sense of rarity and perceived threat.

Sir George Grey Special Collections, Auckland Libraries, AWNS-19090916-4-1
In September 1909 a large adult sea leopard came ashore at Stanmore Bay on the Whangaparoa
Peninsula. It appears that the animal was sadly shot. The Auckland Weekly News image (16 September
1909) shows the Leopard Seal propped up with a small piece of wood the jaws keep apart with a stick
lodged into the mouth.

Despite the evolution of our understanding and the accessibility of information in the internet age, leopard seals in New Zealand continue to face threats. The incident involving Owha in October 2019 stands as a stark reminder. Found bleeding from her face, it was later revealed that she had been shot. Miraculously, she survived the ordeal, but the perpetrator was never identified. This unfortunate event highlighted the persisting challenges and prejudices these creatures face, even in a time when information is readily available.

Similar incidents of leopard seals being shot and killed around the country raise concerns about the protection of wildlife. The minimal punishment for those found guilty of injuring these magnificent creatures adds a layer of urgency to the need for conservation efforts. As the narrative unfolds, it becomes evident that a bridge of understanding between humans and leopard seals is yet to be fully constructed.

My personal journey with Owha began in September 2019, a memory etched in my mind. Responding to a call about a leopard seal in West Harbour Marina, I encountered the playful side of Owha, a trait that didn't always endear her to boat owners. A fender floating in the distance led me along the jetty, where Owha surprised me by emerging from the water just 30 centimetres away. Watching her spy-hop—with her head and upper body above water—revealed the intelligence in her round, beautiful eyes. It was a moment of awe, a realization of the underestimated cognitive abilities of leopard seals.

Her playful antics continued as she demonstrated her affinity for a fender she had playfully removed from a jetty. Over the course of 30 minutes, she would submerge the fender and release it, creating a spectacle akin to a rocket launching from the water. The encounter was my first with a wild leopard seal, a stark contrast to my previous sightings of captive ones at places like Taronga Zoo.

Owha's presence was not a solitary affair; she shared the waters with other leopard seals. Taimana, a young female, found solace in the Gulf during COVID lockdowns, while Pihikete, a young male, lingered for several months in 2023. These additional members of the leopard seal community allowed researchers a rare opportunity to observe and understand the dynamics of these fascinating animals.

The misconceptions surrounding leopard seals were further shattered as Owha continued to engage with the local community. Contrary to the assumption that these creatures are aggressive and solely consume mammals and penguins, Owha showcased a different side. Standing at well over 3 meters in length, she proved to be gentle and exhibited a love for fish rather than bigger prey. People quickly learned that Owha was not to be feared; instead, she was pretty much an honorary citizen of Auckland, weaving herself into the hearts of the community.

Owha relaxing outside the Riverhead Tavern.
Image credit: T Joustra

Her interactions with humans went beyond mere observation. Owha would join people in the water during swimming or diving sessions, following kayaks and surfboards with a playful curiosity that endeared her to most who encountered her (after the original shock of seeing her up close). Despite her size, she became a symbol of grace, challenging preconceived notions about the behaviour of leopard seals.

The culmination of Owha's extended stay in Auckland prompted a wave of research on the species. This newfound understanding contributed to the acknowledgment of leopard seals as a resident species in New Zealand, marking a significant milestone in our evolving relationship with these marine mammals. Owha's presence not only inspired awe and joy but also catalysed scientific exploration and conservation efforts.

My final encounter with Owha, in June 2022 at Bayswater Marina, was bittersweet. Concerns for her health arose after she swallowed fishing line and hooks a few months prior. A collaborative effort resulted in the removal of a substantial sinker and line from her mouth, providing a glimpse into the challenges faced by these creatures in human-dominated environments. Sitting on a pontoon opposite to the pontoon where she lazily sunbathed, I sat and ate my lunch, hoping she was recovering from her latest ordeal. After I left, she disappeared, leaving only memories.

Owha at Westhaven Marina with fishing line and sinker stuck in her mouth. Image credit: T Joustra

As I write this, a year and a half after Owha's last sighting, I reflect fondly on the time she spent in the Hauraki Gulf. Her impact extended beyond the scientific realm; it reached into the hearts of those who witnessed her antics. Owha became a symbol of coexistence, breaking down barriers of fear and misunderstanding. The hope lingers that one day, she might reappear, gracing the shores of Auckland once more.

In essence, Owha's journey in the Hauraki Gulf was a narrative of resilience, wonder, and the delicate balance between human and wildlife interactions. Her story serves as a reminder of the responsibility we bear in protecting and understanding the diverse inhabitants of our planet. As the ripples of Owha's presence continue to be felt, the legacy of this treasured gift from our ancestors lives on, encouraging us to strive for harmony between humanity and leopard seals in the Hauraki Gulf.

Nga Rangi-i-totongia a Tamatekapua

Karen Morris-Denby

**Mahuika, Matoho and Tupua Giants.
Re-imagining a Rangitoto Myth.**

While Goddess of fire *Mahuika*,
slept peacefully through the night,
her fingernails glowed on each breath,
to keep their flickering light.

High on a mountain *Tupua* giants
lived, nestled in the northern shores,
working as always keeping busy,
with their nightly chores.

Wahine Tupua had been weaving,
a magnificent, feathered cloak,
labouring every minute and second,
the fading embers she had forgotten to stoke.

Tupua giants began cursing
screaming, crying like wild beasts,
blaming Mahuika for dousing the fire,
their wailing never ceased.

Being jolted from her slumbers
gave Mahuika such a fright,
she called upon Mataaho God of
earthquakes, it was her given right.
He rattled and shook the mountain
which erupted with a blast,
then hurtled through the floating clouds,
the gulls scattered as it passed.

The mountain landed in the gulf,
which caused a massive wave,
it settled gracefully into the ocean,
as Tupua promised to behave.

The huge crater filled with water,
it swirled and spun around,
this lake named Pupukemoana,
is as beautiful as it sounds.

The mountain settled peacefully.
Now Rangitoto stands supreme.
When mist surrounds the island,
the giants are weeping in their dreams.

Hold

Mayur Wadhwani

"I don't think I am lactose intolerant."

There are certain sentences one shouldn't speak, unless they want to find out how wrong they are. Statements about one's lactose intolerance especially shouldn't be asked while having ice cream in a public space unless one has easy access to a bathroom which they can comfortably destroy. Lastly, if one is making a statement like that to impress a date, this would likely only get a *hmm* sound which means *let's see about that.*

Granted, things were not so dire for Felix. He had easy access to a bathroom, as he was currently standing in the Auckland Ferry Terminal. Additionally, his date Kim has been gelling with him well. He wanted to keep the night going. So when she asked to get some ice cream, he couldn't really refuse. The ferry he had to take to Devonport was scheduled to arrive in the next five minutes and he intended to enjoy his time. But his intestines believed the best way to enjoy time was to push as much as food out as possible.

He did consider the possibility that he was lactose intolerant before he bought an ice cream. He figured that he would have enough time flirt with Kim, say goodbye and get on the ferry. It was quick five minute walk from from Devonport ferry terminal to his home, or a one minute run depending on the urgency. He thought he would be fine. But sometimes, fates are sealed.

Unfortunately for Felix, his fate was decided by a seal. A leopard seal, three meters long and a couple of hundred kilograms heavy had decided that this particular pier of the ferry terminal was going to be his bed for the night, and there's damn near nothing anybody can do about it. After all, the city was only getting out of lockdown so the ferry terminal hadn't been used very much.

Just as Felix swallowed his last spoonful of hokey-pokey ice cream, there was an announcement at the terminal. "Kia ora everyone ..." the announcement began, and Felix had a gut feeling that things were going to down the drain for him. As the announcement continued, passengers at the terminal first grew disgruntled by the delay of the ferry and then bristled with excitement about the idea that a sea creature is nearby.

Kim was one of those people. Her round eyes got larger with cheer and she grabbed his left hand and dragged him to the barricade to see if they could see the seal by the sea. They weren't alone. Beside them, a mother and her child were also trying to do the same thing. The child was moving side to side in an effort to spot the seal. They also tried to push their head through bars but their mother stopped them. Something inside Felix could relate to wanting to get out and not be allowed.

The mother was trying to record a video of the seal, but couldn't get the camera to focus in the dark night. Meanwhile, the child was tugging on the mother's clothes and speaking excitedly.

"Can I pet that dog?"

Kim laughed at the kid and then smiled at Felix before turning back to look at the creature. Felix also saw the animal. Long and fat like a sausage, glistening and wet, slightly brown in the darkness it looked like something that the salt water had expunged. Meanwhile, he could feel the ice cream running down his system, wreaking havoc and gathering dark forces to propel itself towards an eruption. Felix calculated his options. He could use the bathroom in the ferry terminal. But did he really want go and destroy any of them? *Not really*, his brain said while his intestines screamed that there might not be much choice soon and Felix winced.

Kim must have noticed his expression. She came near and asked teasingly "You scared?"

Felix laughed apprehensively, afraid that a fully belly laugh might dislodge some more ice cream down the pipes.

"No, I have seen that seal around before. Totally harmless. But I am 100% sure that the seal does this intentionally," Felix responded.

Kim looked at him in disbelief. "You mean this creature of unknown depths decides that it is bored and wants to annoy some bipeds out on the dry land?"

"Totally" Felix responded. They both chuckled. Kim smiled at him. Felix figured he had a short window of time before the fireworks began so he might as well shoot his shot.

"I enjoyed tonight. I would certainly like to do this again." Kim leaned in closer and gave him a kiss in answer. Felix felt lightheaded and felt butterflies in his stomach. In that moment, he rightfully forgot the impending doom. His abdomen reminded him by imitating whale sounds loudly and Kim pulled away with a raised eyebrow. Felix leaned forward, trying to play it off as if he wanted to continue the kiss but the pained expression gave it away. Another whale sound was emitted and this time Felix had to clench every fibre in his body.

"You know what, I will just go to the bathroom real quick?" Felix pushed the words through his clenched jaw and started walking awkwardly to the bathroom. His steps were quick and but short. Within a few steps he was at the door but much to his dismay, there was an 'Out of Order' sign on the bathroom. He sighed in disappointment but immediately clenched up again.

"Ice cream?" Kim asked in mirth as he came back. Felix couldn't help but feel like the date was ruined, so why bother keeping up the charade.

"And the bathroom is out of order" He complained.

"My office building is right across the road and I can get you in. Do you need it urgently?" Kim offered.

"YES!"

The cheery expression on Kim's face quickly turned serious as she noticed how rapid Felix's walk was. He kept trying to smile at her in thanks but it only came out as a grimace. Kim let him into the PWC building and showed him to the bathroom on the first floor. He ran in. He just hoped that the walls were soundproof.

After committing atrocities to that bathroom, he came out in shame. He all but expected Kim to have left in pity. He tried to see if there's any other exit but much to his dismay, the narrow corridor only went one way - to his embarrassment.

But Kim was still standing there. She smiled when she saw him and there were butterflies in his stomach again. Metaphorically, he hoped.

Secret Selves
Maris O'Rourke

Everyone has a secret self
who turns up to lunch at Mission Bay
in occasional bouts of pāua jandal earrings
purple curls
a dragon tattoo
hidden by a black satin thong

or something scarier
kiss and kick
beaten children too well-loved
stolen cars abandoned at Horopito
smash palace games
home and away

or something exciting
out of bounds
ski trails heading west to a great alpine cirque
beneath a free-yourself sky
holding Lake Alta
deep and tight

Inhabiting the Gap

Alexandra Balm

Between Clarence Rd Eatery and 'Forbidden Arizona'

I don't know why I took such a fancy to this little place by the sea. Just after crossing the Bridge, on the left, on one of the few Queen Streets in Auckland, there's little in the humble frontispiece that says *The Eatery* to announce the peaceful, serene atmosphere inside.

Until a few years ago, the pizza oven flames would warm one side of the T-shaped interior, turning early winter nights into spaces of miracle and wonder. But even after the pizza oven ceased to send its orange reflections on the white walls, *The Eatery* continued to be an enchanted space between work and home, duty and leisure, past and present.

We all need our island of quiet every now and then; our oasis of stillness in the maddening rush around, an objective correlative of a peace of mind we seldom fathom. A place where the loose threads of our lives connect.

I do most of my work preparations in *The Eatery* café near the Bridge, so work doesn't feel like work. I sit at a corner table, from where I can see a stretch of water in the distance, and a good swathe of the sky, quasi-permanently inhabited by clouds.

The Eatery has become a second home. Its cabinet

food—mushroom and cheese pâtés, rocky roads, cheesecakes with berries that bleed crimson into the cream—remind me of the dishes that Mum cooked for birthdays: celeriac and marrow souffle, rum chocolate salami, strawberry and raspberry tart.

The Eatery is my small base from and around which I take walks, either towards the Northcote Tavern or Little Shoal Bay, whenever the moody weather patterns of Auckland permit. I feel at home in the rippling oasis of normalcy along Waitematā Harbour, with its crags, indecently red pōhutukawa, and beaches that shift with the tides and the currents.

Affection offers an illusion of owning, like a child owning their mother. With hardly any family to speak of, I imagine that I am of the land, that I belong, that the past doesn't overshadow the present.

However, on rainy days, when I cannot stroll along the waterfront before settling in to work at my corner table, I cradle a kawakawa tea and think of this other café back in Napoca, Transylvania, the place that I used to call home for decades.

The café was called *Vita Dolce*, though everyone in the city knew it as *Café Arizona*, named after a short story that Bill St. Vergil, a high school student, had written. Bill was fascinated by the literary scene of the city, for which *Vita Dolce* was an impromptu stage. But *Vita Dolce,* and any café, was out of bounds to high school students.

Bill was 17 years old when he wrote his short story, meant to vent his frustration against the late 1950s autocratic state rules that forbade unaccompanied students from entering cafés. This, even though *Vita Dolce* was a place of intellectual and creative effervescence, and therefore a place of educational potential. The story, 'Forbidden Arizona', was tributary, perhaps, to the novels that Bill was reading at the time in his attempt to escape the limitations of a restrictive regime. The story is now lost, but it circulated for months in *samizdat* form. Having been denied the privilege of partaking in the cultural hub of the city, where writers, poets, artists and actors congregated to smoke, drink coffee, gossip and exchange ideas, Bill had compensated by writing his story.

When I met Bill St. Vergil, I was a student, and he a professor and translator. A tall, aging man with a grimace like an eternal smile, and aristocratic mannerisms that did not belong in the communist, yet Balkanic, city of Napoca, he made an impression in any gathering.

'He looks like Anthony Hopkins,' a student said, in a phrase that I couldn't unhear.

St. Vergil taught a class in Modernism—James Joyce, GB Shaw, Katherine Mansfield. During his lectures, he'd read at a slow pace that resembled dictation from a course book that he had written previously, probably in his youth. It was the first volume—the preface announced—of a work that, the Department librarians insisted, had never been followed by a second.

I was a third-year student, overwhelmed by coursework that required us to be in the library or lecture halls from 8 am to 8 pm, with a couple of hours break for lunch. When we complained that, all up, we had to read and respond to 40 novels per semester, Professor St. Vergil's reaction was, 'You are young. You can do it.'

And we did.

Without being dictatorial, whatever he said went. He was always calm, with an equipoise that commanded attention. Although most of his students were women, there was no gossip about him, no racy stories. Most looked up to him as a father figure.

When my father was working in Italy for a couple of years, I missed him so acutely that the only times when I wasn't sulking were when I attended Professor St. Vergil's classes. He created an atmosphere of wellbeing around him, like an aura that softened spikes and polished sharp, hard edges. I grew to believe that there might be an evolution in allowing the shells of selfhood to become porous or permeable and think of one's teachers or lecturers, of one's city, of one's world as family.

Whenever I visited Napoca, I made a point of calling Professor St. Vergil to arrange a coffee meeting. Seeing him became a regular fixture of my short visits home. He was part of the city, as were my parents and friends, school and university mates, the river, and the city centre buildings with their mix of Art Nouveau, Viennese, and Gothic styles.

He was a local legend, the way he listened to everyone patiently, from caretakers to deans, obscure writers to celebrities. He smiled at human folly and offered support. He was a bit of a saint, the way he sailed and glided rather than walked the narrow medieval city streets, his light-coloured eyes observing the human comedy divine from the height of his Viking-like stature.

When my father died, I met Professor St. Vergil at *Arizona* a few days after the funeral.

'I'm so sorry for your loss,' he said in a soft tone as he shook my hand. He'd given up the Levantine kissing of women's hands a few years prior, as had most men in Napoca.

'Your father was a good man,' he added.

'I never knew that you had met him,' I said.

'I saw him once or twice when he was a young lecturer. He made quite an impression. A good man,' he repeated. 'I wish I'd known your mother better, too.'

Oh, is there a tinge of nostalgia in his voice? I wondered.

'Did you know that nostalgia was considered a disease in the seventeenth century?' he asked, as if he could read my mind. 'Johannes Hofer, a young Swiss doctor, just nineteen years old, coined the term to talk about an ailment that afflicted mercenaries fighting far from home. Not too different from homesickness.'

'How quaint! If nostalgia were a disease, in these days of mass migrations and displacements, half the people in the world would be sick,' I quipped.

'Perhaps they are,' he said, half smiling.

'Perhaps we are,' I said, echoing his words.

'There are people, though, who could cure such malaise,' he said. 'Your mother's such a person. Though she was very young when I met her, I could see a spark of the spirit in her. She emanated a sense of peace, of wellbeing, of homeliness. Each time I met her it felt like a return home.'

'Well, I'm starting to see that side of her, too,' I said.

'She didn't talk a lot, but she wasn't morose. She resembled a calm lake that reflected a light bigger than itself.'

'How strange to think that knowledge of the spirit used to be forbidden in some cultures,' I mused.

'Well, personal emancipation can lead to subverting systems of power,' he said.

We were quiet for a while. A shaft of light, reflected from a window across the street, nestled for a few seconds on his right shoulder, as if conferring a symbolic knighthood.

Arizona was rather empty at the time. It was late morning, a Tuesday on the third week of the academic year when students attended every single lecture, seminar or lab. The literary hub of the city that Bill St. Vergil had involuntarily become godfather to in his youth felt deserted. The staff treated him with reverence and respect that bordered on affection. There were none of the dismissive, threatening attitudes that the erstwhile high school student would have faced when he risked being stood down for entering the café.

We sat at a corner table from where we could see the whole of *Arizona* and the street it was on. We talked about books and common acquaintances while people, dressed in autumnal greys, ochres and browns, rolled past the windows. Near the entrance, in a linden tree, a few yellow leaves were still hanging stubbornly from otherwise barren branches. I looked at the man in front of me and wondered how my life would have been had I had a different father.

He mentioned authors that he'd translated: Joseph Conrad, Margaret Atwood, Toni Morrison. I mentioned my antipodean adventures, not climbing Aoraki Mount Cook—mountains are to be worshipped, not climbed—swimming in the Pacific Ocean, camping at the foothills of snow-covered mountains, kayaking in labyrinthine mangrove lows.

'I'd like you to have this,' Professor St. Vergil said, as we stood up to leave. We had been talking for a couple of hours. He proffered a purple-cover book. 'It's one of my latest translations: *Beloved*,' he added, his left hand on my forearm.

I shook his hand, risked a hug, then hurried out of *Arizona*. The once-smoky café where my father would buy me a box of assorted cookies, redolent of tobacco smoke, whenever we walked past, released me from its grip. I didn't miss my father yet. *Somehow, he's still around,* I thought. The city had a strange way of entangling our stories.

Shortly afterward *Arizona* was closed.

I visited Napoca last in the winter of 2020, before the pandemic. I managed to meet Professor St. Vergil in the wagon-like room of *Carpathians*, a café around the corner from where *Arizona* had been. We shared stories and cradled cappuccinos, we laughed at a joke that I cannot remember now. When it was time to leave, he helped me into my winter coat before he put on his own, always the gentleman despite the slight tremor of his hands.

We ambled towards the building of the University around the corner. Where *Arizona* once stood, there's now a kebab place. Through the colourless window, we contemplated the carefully groomed, trim middle-aged women sitting next to balding, overweight men. I turned to Professor St. Vergil and smiled.

'This reminds me of a Katherine Mansfield short story,' I said. With a hand on my shoulder, he smiled back. He could read me, as my father used to.

We said our goodbyes. As he continued towards the University building, I remembered my mom's remark a few days after my father had died.

'For all your attachment, for all the mannerisms that you copied from him, you are not only your father's daughter.'

I never saw Professor St. Vergil again.

I go to *The Eatery* whenever I miss innocent interactions with non-judgemental people. In a café, like in a train station or an airport, we pass through each other's lives so fast that judging or applying labels is not worth the effort. Before or after a coffee or a light meal, I walk along the streets overlooking the Hauraki Gulf with its pocket-sized beaches and pōhutukawa laden with flowers, carrying my stories with me. Every now and then, I launch them on the still waters, hoping that one day someone will find them, and that we'll then be friends.

Pōhutukawa beach. Image: Melissa Gunn

Motu

Angela Campbell

"You" dwells between sleep and awake,
between sound and silence.
"You" is the break and the swell -
the scream and the lullaby.

Ungraspable and ill-defined, just like me.

"We" drifted the tide of our many lives,
creating hope from hopeless histories,
floating between hauora and hell.
"We" was the fever in which I longed to dream.

Now, my love, I'm quite the realist...

Between us are all the great and little barriers.
Between us is a never-conceived son
and grandchildren with molten chocolate eyes,
the dozen proposals that happened,
and the anniversaries that didn't.

Between us is beauty run rampant—countless waltzing waves,
pōhutukawa needles, adrift on warm winds,
the wine we never drank,
the boat we never sailed,
the summer we never became.

I know now, my love, that I am Leigh
and you are Port Jackson.

We are the edges of the Gulf.

We share only tides these days
and we're both just fine, I guess…

Reaching toward each other
but not for each other,
always looking inward
united by what divides us.

Calm and Chaos. Image: Susan Glamuzina

Ocean

Edna Heled

We had a rough sleepless night, you and I
out my window I sensed you hiding your whales so well
veiling from me as I toss and turn to ride your force

Thrown out from the most sacred mountain on earth
a flake on the map that draws the world's fiercest spirits -
it's the vastness of your foam that comforts my days

While, breathless, I try to chase parallel universes
your waves reach my roots far back in the mount I am planted
connect my infinite branches to the cosmic light

Ocean, my ocean, forever remind me
You are my arms, my voice, my gaze, my eternity
I don't need to see you to know you are with me

When I long to Zion I can just listen
the deep swamp of the south is becoming my coffer
there is no silence that doesn't end

Ocean. Oil on canvas. 600x600. Edna Heled

Becoming Rangitoto

Darian Smith

I leave her behind. The love of my life. I leave her trapped in her prison and I come to a place of couples and families. But I am alone.

I am a spot of darkness on the light, golden sand. No one sees it but me. They think I'm one of them. I look like them and I smile. I even walk as they do but I know it for what it is. I squish my toes into the sand, curling them, squeezing them, feeling the strength of muscle and tendon in every movement. I do not take those movements for granted. I've seen how easily they are taken.

This bay is a happy place. The sun sparkles on the water. Children laugh and play on the grass between the sand of the beach and the shops beyond. The threshold between the regular world and the ocean. Between regular people and... me.

A couple run side by side past the fountain in his-and-hers jogging shorts. They match their pace. They'd be holding hands if they could. Young love. Married, I suppose. Training for Round the Bays or perhaps just to stay fit. They will have vowed "In sickness and in health." They have the health. They don't know about sickness yet. Not really. Nobody does until it happens.

I turn away from that world of shops and families and runners, all shining with ignorant bliss and the confidence that their bodies are reliable. Trustworthy. Safe. They are not.

My eyes seek Rangitoto, rising out of the water. His slopes are solid, stable. Strong. Rangitoto could hold up the sky when it is weak and crying. Rangitoto carries ecosystems on his back. Rangitoto has seen death, pain and shattering eruption, and lives on. I'm drawn to that strength. I need it.

I walk across the sand she can no longer walk on without falling. I let the water touch my skin. The chill of it moves up over my ankles and calves, creeping up my legs in a tide of paralysis. Is this what it is like for her? To have pieces of her body stop working? To lose control inch by inch?

I move my legs and walk deeper. The cold reaches my heart. Thud. Thud. Ice.

I stare at the horizon. A tsunami is coming though the water is still. It is bigger every day. More of her lost, betrayed by her own body.

The wave hits and takes me under. I tumble, disoriented and confused. The world no longer solid. I'm washed away, unable to change it. Unable to stop it. I'm drowning. Wounded and hurting yet healthy and unharmed. Overwhelmed by losses that are not my own. I can still walk on the sand. I can still run. But not with her.

Not unless I carry her. Not unless I am strong. Even while drowning.

Rangitoto rises from the water and I go home.

Blood Protectors - Rosie

Sue Carpenter

Rosie

Everybody tries to make the most of their life, taking up opportunities, reaching for goals. This is even more so when your life has a span of only seven days. Buzzing around downtown Auckland, I'm focused on my goal of finding my Blood. For us mosquitoes, one human's Blood could enhance and prolong our lives, we just have to find that one. As a group of teenagers board a ferry, so do I. We haven't even left the wharf before I find her.

The ride isn't too long or rough to Rangitoto Island as I stow away inside the cabin, watching my Blood from a distance. If my wings get water on them, I won't be able to fly till they are dry again and could lose her. If I lose her after seven days, I won't be able to transform and will not get to live a longer life. So long as I taste my Blood's blood every seven days, I live until she dies.

The school kids, teachers and parents jump off the ship, gathering their gear, and walk along a track to the next island over – Motutapu Island. Some girls have only been walking for ten minutes when they start complaining about the dust all around. I don't have an issue flying through dust, and my Blood is with a group of boys laughing. She chats the whole time without a worry or complaint.

They trot off over a quaint wooden bridge and up a steep hill where I'm amazed by the view over the Hauraki Gulf to Great Barrier Island and the Coromandel. When I transformed to her Blood Protector all her information was gifted to me. Now, like her, I know the names of the islands around us but when the teacher says we have 1,000 meters to walk I have no idea if that's a long way or not.

One girl trips over as she falls down the steep hill, my Blood stops to help her. Thankfully I have a kind human Blood.

I observe her as she arrives at camp and settles in. They are put into groups, camp set up, and they start activities. Building a raft with barrels, which tips over and sinks to splashes and laughter, they all get wet. Most of the girls scream at all the activities, not my Blood. She laughs with her friends. When they are snorkelling, the leader opens a kina, causing lots of fish to swim around snacking. Then kayaking, and an obstacle course with a zip line where if they lose focus, they fall in mud. The next day they climb pillars with a harness and have to do a star jump at the top, which most students don't do. She does. Orientation is the last activity before lunch. During the free time, the girl that had fallen over asks my Blood to go for a walk with her and they find a gun emplacement. The two girls sneak in to look and the tripped over girl closes the door on her friend and runs off laughing. My Blood had helped her. I was about to change and open the door when three other girls appear laughing.

'Help,' my Blood screams from inside.

Little shits, I leave and buzz off to get a teacher, but first I need clothes.

Ruby

Always my luck, every time I think a girl is nice, she flips. I wouldn't care if I wasn't claustrophobic. 'Let me out, please.' The space is getting smaller and darker by the second. I lie down at the crack by the bottom of the door, breathing in the fresh air. Aside from the ringing in my ears, I can hear cackling. Why won't they pick on someone else, just once? I had been having the time of my life. I push against the door and the hinged side moves a little. I push with all my strength and it gives a little more. The hinges are rusted – perfect. I stand up and do a giant kick like my friend Danny had taught me. Pow! The door falls off and I climb out, covered in dirt from the ground.

The girls stop laughing as I charge at them.

'The mud monster's gonna get us,' one screeches.

I pick up more mud and charge at them. I quickly catch up, and rub dirt and grass in their hair and on their clothes.

'Stop it!' Mrs Johnston calls.

'Enough!' shouts the school dean.

I grab dirt and throw it at them as Mr Dunlop, the headmaster picks me up and throws me over his shoulder. This doesn't stop me kicking and punching the air. 'Put me down Dad, I can hold my own.'

'I know. I am proud of you.'

'How did you know?'

'The girl in the white told us.' We looked where he pointed.

'What girl?' I ask looking at the teachers. There are only the two other teachers but there is a white dress on the ground. I run away from dad and charge towards the water to get clean.

'What happened?' Avi asks, diving in after me. 'Not telling yet,' I say.

'You're never calm.' Ian laughs diving in too.

'Wish I was a guy,' I say, 'then they wouldn't tease me.'

'They still would Ruby, you are the headmaster's kid.'

The mean girls come down to the water's edge dirty, the boys all laugh at them. As they dip their toes in the water, they scream saying it's too cold.

'Clean yourself, girls,' Dad says, so they all dunk under the surface, re-emerging clean as quick as possible and run off to the dorms. I know they will be putting something in my sleeping bag. Two of them are in my cabin group.

Rosie

I have almost been seen by my Blood, that's against the rules, I have to be more careful. I watch as the human toads put a frog in my Blood's sleeping bag, poor frog, but hey, it would eat me in my natural form if it got half a chance so as a human I find more and put them in all the mean girls' sleeping bags. Transformed, I buzz into the corner watching over everyone. Whatever the girls try to do to Ruby, I save the day. Spaghetti in Ruby's pillowcase; I cleaned it and put spaghetti in their pillowcases, unseen by all. I take the laces out of their shoes, as they do everything to ruin her trip but fail each time. I love a challenge and being Ruby's Blood Protector is going to be fun. They will never hurt her again.

Matariki morning. Image: Melissa Gunn

The Ineffable

Marguerite Laing

Sinking into delicious drowsiness
familiar edges soften
dreams nudge and spill into consciousness
as the infinite melts into now

Perhaps communion of these utterly separate realms
occurs only in mystical devotion, caritas
or, pure unadulterated love

Or, does it dwell
longing to be discovered
in those tiny filaments of awareness
between sleeping and waking
between living and dying
between ephemeral glimmers of paradise
and the endless morass of samsara

Storm II. Marguerite Laing

Jim, the Old Man of the Hauraki

Sarah Valentine

Prologue

Wind whipped around Sam, trying to slap the lines out of his sun-browned, nimble grasp. The sea, yesterday a multi-faceted jewel, today frothed and seethed as it slapped at the hull. He watched as Gem finished lashing the tender to the railing and scanned the shoreline, straining his ears to listen as she turned towards him and yelled. Her words were ripped apart by Tāwhirimātea.

"E hoa… that old Jim down… the wharf? Think we oughta tell 'im … storm brewing?"

Sam's smile was a grimace as he hauled the last of the mainsail into position and safely lashed her down before grabbing Gem's arm and pulling her closer.

"Don't fuss. Jim's as tough as they come," he shouted towards her ear. "And that dinghy might look like trash, but she'll surprise you. That man goes out every day and always comes home. The Hauraki's got his back."

Jim saw them watching. Especially young Gem. He'd seen her grow up. He knew about her. She was like a scallop, rough and tumble on the outside, but soft at heart. He raised his hand in greeting. Perhaps it would ease her concern, if she could see it through the pelting rain.

"Okay old girl. Tāwhirimātea's a grumpy old fart today."

Jim always talked to Pūtohe, his dinghy, out loud. He knew every knot in her wood, every groan and squeak she made. Knew where to put his weight to avoid putting too much stress on her bolts. In his eyes her rust-red, streaky paint was still bright crimson.

He pulled hard at the cord on her 30-horsepower outboard motor and listened as she coughed into life.

"Let's go, old girl," he said, urging her into a canter through the slapping whitecaps. "He'll let us know if it's time to come in."

These days, Jim brought old Moggie, his cat, out with him. His ears weren't what they used to be, and she could listen for the slap. The Hauraki looked after its own, and Jim knew that The Flounder would slap Pūtohe's hull when it was time to come in. It always had. Moggie meowed quietly in her raincoat. She was the best girl, but she still hated the rain. Jim laid his hand on her back, and she half closed her eyes.

The slap came when Jim had just finished his haul. Two fish were enough for today. One to eat and one for the old boy next door.

"Alright girl," Jim murmured to Moggie. "Let's head for home. Come on, Pūtohe, let her rip."

The coastline swirled and warped through the storm. Dark shadows raged towards them, screaming and howling. Salt and brine filled the nostrils and ears. Jim eased Pūtohe back.

"Easy girl, let's all get home today."

Moggie howled as one shadow roared louder than the storm. A speed boat, heading away from the wharf.

"That was Mac's boat, Moggie. Probably his darn twins. Come on, let's go tell 'em." He turned Pūtohe, pushed the throttle hard, and let her gallop.

Pelting rain blinded him, the wind whipped through one ear

and out the other, turning his brain into a drum. Senses were no longer worth relying on—only muscle memory. In the moment after wiping his eyes, Jim saw the boat in front skid around the corner, careening over before righting herself. Stupid kids. Jim had to swerve like he was trying to flick a kid off a towed biscuit when he finally rounded the headland and they were sitting just there. There was a triangle here, tucked behind the wooded cliff face that was part-sheltered. Jim sucked his teeth and cleared his throat.

"Oi twins! What would your father say?" he yelled. "Does he know you have his boat?" Jim put his hand on Moggie to calm her frantic meows. It was time to go.

A round teenage face appeared to port, wet and shiny. She squinted at him and burst out laughing.

"Syrus, it's that old guy, the weird one with the cat," she called.

The second twin appeared, this one with a scowl dripping off his face.

"Get outta here old man. Can't you see there's a storm?" yelled Syrus.

"I know that, you muffin-head! You need to head back in. The Hauraki's warning us, sending us home. Turn that boat around and GET!" Jim was trembling now, his vocal cords aching from the strain.

"Stop horsing it old man! Leave us alone. We know what we're about," shouted the girl, and Mac's boat roared into life.

Moggie was insistent now. Clawing the bench, the hull, his leg. Danger was close. Tangaroa wanted Tāne's children.

"Okay, okay, I'm paying attention." Jim put his hand on Moggie's back and let Pūtohe splutter back into life. This was cutting it too fine, but those kids... he couldn't take his eyes off them. Tāwhirimātea stole them from view, breaking the spell. Pūtohe reared into gear and they cantered back towards the wharf.

"When did the young'uns forget how to listen?" He groaned as they picked their way between the squalls, using a bucket to shed the rainwater before they sunk.

Jim refused to read the local rag for the next few days. The news found him though, through the mouth of young Gem.

"You joinin' the search, Jim?" she asked, as he wriggled Moggie's raincoat on to her.

"The search?" He asked, half a whisper.

"Yeah, you know, those twins e hoa? Mac's youngest tamariki."

Jim sucked his teeth and swung his legs nimbly into Pūtohe, avoiding the splinters Moggie had pulled up. He'd sand the seat back, later.

"Guess I am," he said. "Come on old girl."

Sea Spray. Acrylic on canvas. Melissa Gunn

Captain Cook in the City

Julie Ryan

He catches a free bus to the city.
It trawls up and down streets for trade
between the million-dollar houses
and past magnificent straddle cranes
at Santa Claus' depot stacked with goodies.
Alights at Britomart, opposite Queens Wharf
where a monstrous cruise ship's docking.

He hurries to the front berth, discovers
a solitary state house, plonked.
This astounding worker's residence
has absolute waterfront views,
but not a stick of furniture except
a table on which he sits, dangling his shoes.

He examines the wonders spiders have wrought
in dazzling colour – they always claim droit de seigneur.
One scrawl resembles his chart of the coast.

He imagines the weary worker each night
as he mounts his own staircase -
the wife descending next morning like a princess,
with enigmatic smile and a laundry basket.

Somehow the upper walls reflect the city outside,
skies, ships, houses, clock towers.
"So this is what I came forth to see:
a Workers Paradise."

Harbour lights. Image: Susan Glamuzina

Fisherman's Hobby

Rina Patel

Suddenly, there it is: Rangitoto
Surrounded by a deep green tutu, the Hauraki Gulf.

One dude madly steers at the speed of Sonic the
Hedgehog.

Our butts have been rhythmically bouncing
up down, up down.
To the splash bash and crash
of this water taxi's hull,
bumping and smacking, wavy mass after mass.
Four sun-kissed faces welcoming sporadic sprays of
ocean.
Our salty hair blowing in all manner of directions.
Ceiling speakers bellowing 'You're Simply The Best' into
the bright blue sky.

Drastically the engine gear drops.
We glide...then drift.
Land comes pulling in,
the port of Auckland enlargens, inch by inch.

The comforting veil of summer holiday lifts, revealing:

cruddy empty plastic bottles, strewn bits of fishing nylon, numerous overhanging rods, a random grotty filleting knife, and one small silvery smudged handbasin full of bachelor's carelessness.

Right o, we are just this fisherman's hobby!

We dock,
returning back to our JAFA selves - secretly longing for slow, hot showers.
Up the timber ramp we go, dragging bulky luggage, clickety-clacking, rickety-ricketing
until we hit the burrrrr of polyurethane wheels on concrete.
We cross a lifetime's worth of white lines and tarmac.
The growing weight of reality tugs.
It's a couple days after New Years and who wants be parked up anywhere?

Then: *hallelujah*
a shiny black stallion stands before us,
beckoning our city slicker need to be raced home in full leather comfort.
The oversized beast has been idling longer than a full e-car charge.

The stocky Gen Z cuzzy steps down donning his fresh
new red plaid shirt.
Proudly yanking the boot wide open,
he greets us by bumping in clumpy bag after bag upon
bag...
Belts click, the AC continues blasting full tilt through all
the wide open windows.
Goodbye summer holiday, hello CBD hell,
sun is shining, make you want to move your dancing feet.

Image: Rina Patel

Tribute to Sailor James St Claire Rolton - Tune to Drunken Sailor

AGE Virtual LC

What shall we do with a wayward pirate?
What shall we do with a wayward pirate?
What shall we do with a wayward pirate?
From Hauraki Gulf History!
Right up the centre of the Firth
Damn straight, up the mighty Firth
First Englishman sailing up the Firth
From Hauraki Gulf History!
Twinkle in his eye
Dimple in his chin
Lovely lassies drawn to him
Rogue of the Thames
Dashing daring Drake
From Hauraki Gulf History!
What shall we do with the scoundrel of the seas?
What shall we do with the scoundrel of the seas?
What shall we do with the scoundrel of the seas?
From Hauraki Gulf History!
Wife and family follow him over
Gang bridge lowers
Petticoat captured
around the oars

Traps her in a death knell
Drowns
in
the
bottom
of
the
sea.
What shall we do with a motherless family?
What shall we do with a motherless family?
What shall we do with a motherless family?
From Hauraki Gulf History!
Marry the nanny
Fast quick to it
Ring on her finger
Don't reject it
Come on me lovely
You're the new momma
From Hauraki Gulf History!
Right up the centre of the Firth
Damn straight, up the mighty Firth
First Englishman sailing up the Firth
From Hauraki Gulf History!

The Hauraki Gulf

Elijah Foxwell

The Hauraki Gulf
a special place
A way to spend your summer days,
frolicking about,
messing around,
on such a beautiful summer's day
I want to be where
the sun shines bright,
the wind blows strong,
the ships honk,
the birds wail,
Joy lives.
The Hauraki Gulf

Kererū Taonga of Gulf Harbour

Conrad Mende

Pirate of the Hauraki Gulf ocean of trees
Collects a bounty of berries
Gobbling them down greedily
Chug
Glug
Burp
Berries fermenting
building a sense of festivity
Bright mulled berries sitting, waiting, brewing
Plop
Plonk
Thud

Image: Conrad Mende

Long Bay Before New Normal

Charlie Wang

I remember when visiting Long Bay Beach was so normal, for me and my family. A beautiful bay, where my heart sang and my soul felt free. The feeling of walking barefoot through the silky sand, as it slipped between my toes, made me giggle. That salty sand had been washed around the Hauraki Gulf, by the ocean waves, for millions of years. Tiny ancient particles dried on my feet and once washed away left my tiptoes smooth and soft like a pebble.

Watching the cool surf rush in and out was interesting to walk through and allowed me time to think and ponder about so many things. I was excited to be outdoors, I loved being with my family, I loved watching Oreo running away from the hungry waves. I wanted this moment in time to never end.

The view was extraordinary. Millions of shiny shells surrounded me. If I could have dived into those curly conical shells and listened, for hours on end, to the ocean waves I would have. So much peace, so much stillness, so much time to simply be me.

Large pōhutukawa buzzing with the sound of busy bees drifted along the breeze. Savoury sausages sizzling on BBQ's, hiding behind large, tall trees, smelt so good, my mouth waters even now recalling this part of the day. I kind of miss some parts of being around other humans.

Playground screeches, screams and laughter also filled the air, to be fair the dogs barking like parrots and children hooting like owls was pretty unsettling. I like things quiet, slow and steady. That's me, I'm like the flotsam and jetsam of the sea.

Long Bay Beach has not changed; well maybe it has, I am not there, I am here, online, learning.

Albatross. Lucas Glamuzina

Artwork by Mt Albert Rangers

Amelia Barr

Megan Arthur

Isla McLellan

Keira Bailie

Isla O'Shannessy

Artwork by AGE Virtual Learners

Birds of Tiritiri Matangi.
Photo credit: Conrad Mende

Island escape -
Ship Wreck Island
Flotsam and jetsam
collage by
PJ and AJ Wrathall.

Photo credit: Bron van der Geest

Journey to Motuihe

Elise Cater

Pipeo was walking around town, looking for bakeries or apothecaries, when she discovered a magical workshop. Dried herbs like malcrop root, sheep's ivy, and lavender hung from the ceiling or were scattered over the bench snaking around the walls. She walked in. The owner claimed she could make fluffy, bubbly, clouds appear out of nowhere to drift around in the air.

"I'm sure your dragon would like to fly without having to flap his wings," she encouraged.

"Thanks, but I'm here for something specific. Do you have any sweet roots or dried field moss?" Pipeo asked.

"This side of the Hauraki? You'll have to go further north for that."

Pipeo started to reach for Cress, when the shopkeeper hastily added,

"But I do have some Meadowbell if that'll do?" She didn't want to lose a customer.

"Yes please, Meadowbell will prove useful; it's going to be a challenge getting the ingredients I'm after." A bit more than a challenge, actually, Pipeo thought to herself. Having to stop for Cress to rest and eat, along with any rough terrain we may encounter. And that's just if we don't get tricked by wild Floofas. Those little creatures are always trying to steal things and cause mischief.

"Well, I can't guarantee it, but there should be some good herbs on Motuihe. Of course, if you need any equipment to get there...?" She was still trying to make sales.

It wouldn't hurt to have some supplies though, Pipeo reflected. So she gathered her purchases and set off for Motuihe Island.

The waves crashed fiercely along the shoreline. Pipeo dragged her rowboat painstakingly through the sand. She hauled it to the surf and pushed it into the water. As she heaved her oars backwards and forwards she became increasingly aware of the sea's choppiness. The sky had darkened on her way to the beach, and was now threatening to rain down on her.

Wind was sweeping across the surface of the water, stirring it up like a giant cup of tea. The waves were rising higher and higher; the island was getting closer, but not fast enough for Pipeo to escape the storm. Suddenly the whole boat lurched as it hit a rock protruding from the ocean floor. Torrents engulfed the rowboat, crashing over the deck, snatching Pipeo away from her seat and tossing her about in the current. She could feel her loose tunic and boots being tugged at from below, dragging her down, away from fresh air. Oh why did I go to an island? I should've just found a shop further north. Her stomach churned with misgiving.

She fought against the invisible forces pulling her down until her head burst into the air above so that she could take a gasping breath. Living beside a river certainly has its uses, Pipeo thought. Being a strong swimmer is very helpful. Slowly but surely, she made her way to the island, flopping down on the sandy beach to rest with a sigh of relief.

Grandmother Pōhutukawa, Thank You

AJ Wrathall

Grandmother Pōhutukawa thank you
Thank for your
crinkly crooked
branches
they keep me safe
Thank you for your
rough
weathered bark
my tiny finger holds
Thank you Grandmother Pōhutukawa
for letting me play
holding my mum

her mum
And
Me

The Deep Dark Ocean

Frankie Glamuzina

water presses
dark blue
surrounds eyes
as you kick
down into the darkness

Three Hour Tour

Patricia Gilmour

A three-hour tour around the Gulf
Wild, stormy weather
The waves came up rapidly
The captain, first mate, the power couple,
An A-list actress, a doctor and his girlfriend
Surging, turbulence and fear.

In the eye of the storm
Eerily quiet...
Mayday! Mayday!

Exhaustive four-hour search
Emergency services despatched
Coastguard vessels and Westpac helicopter

Radio silence, the boat not located -
No sightings within the Hauraki Triangle,
All seven aboard, presumed lost.

Found twenty-four hours later
Safely ashore since the night before.
Today, another gorgeous day on the Gulf.

Stormy day. Image: Melissa Gunn

The Greatest Catch

Shan Iyer

Once upon a summer Auckland day
Upon a cloudless day under the humid, beating sun
Our family drove to the nearest vast ocean-blue
Our whanau packed our bags for the Hauraki Gulf bay
As we speed across the grey lands, crawling like ants
Into the crystal waters, we sunk down together.
In scientifically advanced engineered water suits
The secret seas, we larked around.
Subsuming further downwards for our unspoken prey
Nearest by the current gushed streams seabed
Sighting snappers, jellyfish and other exotic fishes
Our aim was for his dead carcasses to feast.
For here, the defiant King Mako secretly dwelled
At the bottom of the Hauraki deep
Like a monstrous pale Taniwha,
His eyes gleamed icy white.
As we gathered our mahi, all fear disappeared.
We fanned out, spearing his robust belly.
Yet together, we pressed onward with our assault
He put up a battling fight, yet with spears
We were all so well-prepared
The glistening ivories with the sharpest array of teeth

Yet soon, we pierced his side and the ocean bloodied.
The blood clouded green, his eyes transfixed in shock
A pained-in, ungodly ghostly pale hue
Across the Hauraki sandy beach
We returned like clawing crabs.
To the docks amidst a new sea of gathered reporters
Soon, warm shots were snapped by waiting newspaper reps
Recording the day for Tāmaki Makaurau citizens
We held our puffed chests, hands proud and smiling.
As we presented the gigantic carcass
Over thirty kilograms in weight
A catch unsurpassed in all imaginations
Our flesh trophy won from the gaudy chaos
What did Hauraki spew up?
In all records past belief
Our three names are etched as records in the halls of fame.
The greatest catch from the alluring Hauraki Gulf
The world has never imagined or seen.

Treasure Hunter. Image: Melissa Gunn

Hauraki Gulf Unsung Hero

Bron van der Geest

Tiritiri Matangi Island
Hauraki Gulf
New Zealand
23/01/24

Dear Mr Galbraith,

My heart soared today as I scanned the verdant, sage, khaki, olive, emerald and turquoise hues of flora that bedecks Tiritiri Matangi Island. I smiled reminiscing about those seeds of hope, your passion sowed in teenager hearts, many years ago in the 80's, regarding ways to influence positive change across Aotearoa. What resonated for me was the way in which the joy of your thinking lit up your eyes and although it was tricky to work out what your face was pondering, at times, as that big bushy beard covered so much of it, your eyes could never hide the truth of your communication. We certainly were not the best nor the worst of teenagers but the way you discussed and shared your world with us made us feel like equals.

My brother and I looked at each other today and sighed in synchronicity, for your living legacy, your ideation, spread far and wide across the nooks and crannies of this tiny jewel in our Hauraki Gulf. So many students took up the mantle to run with your dare to dream, collectively spreading seeds across the landscape.

I reached out via social media too, checking in with teenage hearts, now mature men and women, laughing, giggling and crying as we reminisced about that back breaking action, digging, weeding, planting, repeat, digging, weeding, planting repeat.

We searched for details about you in every word filled space on the island, and then tucked away at the bottom of a display panel, we found a teeny tiny photo capturing the top of your head, doing what you loved best, being a kaitiaki. No fuss, no big bold larger than life presentation, with fanfare extolling your greatness. To be fair, you probably did not want this thumbnail offering either, not at all your scene.

Your eulogy in 2018, to another extraordinary human, keen to lead the charge, expressed your fascination about the possibilities of what Tiritiri Matangi could be. You lit this fire of fascination in the hearts of many. You see, my daughter too played her part as a young wonder digging, weeding, planting, repeat, digging, weeding, planting repeat, at Shakespear Regional Park to assist our native feathered friends on their navigation across the great divide.

Mr Galbraith, without your vision, commitment and dedication the gift of greenery would not be so prevalent, I suspect. And it is crucial that your passion, which was passed onto ourselves, is ignited in the baton sharing of our future generations. The Hauraki Gulf probably has many unsung heroes and you, to me, are most assuredly one. Your ability to be an undercover maestro helped me develop my facilitation style and teaching practice, absolutely gold!

Your light may now be gone from us, but your "river of trees" runs wild: from Tiritiri Matangi to the Waitākere Ranges.

Gone but not forgotten.

Yours gratefully

Bron van der Geest (nee Gurney)

Picture-book perfect. Kawau Island. Image: Gary van der Geest

Patupaiarehe

Brian Evans

The perfumed sails of evening
rose gently o'er the sand
where drying nets and wooden boats
lay freed from human hands
the tide relaxed its restless roam
and lowed in dark repose
a boy and girl came near to stare
and to breathe the sweet sea air
they kissed and Patupaiarehe lights
streaked through that Waiheke sea
oh teeming sprights!
Oh feral mites
So old! So young! So free
side by side those lovers dived
we swam with the Patupaiarehe!

What do to in an Emergency

Gretchen Carroll

Remain calm and take a deep breath.

We loaded the car with our bags and piled in, dreading the traffic home. The kids started complaining about an annoying fly, which persistently buzzed and dive-bombed them.

If you are not sure whether emergency services are needed, call anyway.

The benefit of being on holiday is that you can avoid the news. But in the car, we heard on the radio that the Australian bush fires were raging on and on. We quickly switched to a David Walliams audio book for the younger passengers' sake. Or ours.

Always send for help as soon as possible.

Driving through the green pastures, it was hard to imagine all this engulfed in fire. As we crossed the Harbour Bridge and looked out to the beleaguered Hauraki Gulf, the light started to change. I lowered my sunglasses and the window. It wasn't a problem with my eyes.

Once you have made contact, LISTEN carefully and answer the questions.

"The sky's changed colour!""Why is it so orange?""Is Auckland on fire?""No, it's the smoke blowing over from Australia.""It's so crazy, it feels like night-time.""Yeah, it's weird."

If you feel you are unable to do anything, send for help.

Standing in our driveway, I felt as though we'd landed on another planet. Or arrived in a dystopian future, the one we have all read about but think we still have time to avoid.

Remain calm and take a deep breath.

Rangitoto from Takapuna. Image: Denise T O'Hagan

Adrift

Alexandra Fraser

The kayak drifts over drowned
mangroves   seaweed like hair

You are lost   displaced in place
floating   look back to the city

evening tide full   smooth
a mirrored gloss

reflects each coloured light
each concrete spar

thin layer to hold the city's quanta
one gust of wind   the city is gone

and you hang on
fingers bruised   nails breaking

the tide will last as long as the moon
licking   dissolving   undercutting

What Will I Do?

Lee Simpson

We all have skills and one of mine is finding my way around inside dark houses. I gained this skill in Palmy when I was studying banking at university but now, I only navigate the two houses in the dark—Gavin's and mine. He and I have a complicated relationship. He's often out of town and doesn't like phones, so whenever we run into each other, I go home with him.

My twenty-fifth birthday is coming up and I have decided I'm old enough to have a serious relationship and next time I see Gavin I'm going to ask him to come as my date to my party. It will be low-key, my parents, flatmate, and him. Tammy doesn't like Gavin—she thinks he is using me—but I have been with Gavin on and off for five years, I went to uni and saw other people and he's been off and seen others but like magnets, we always end up together again. And now it's time to commit.

I get up for the third time tonight to navigate in the dark to the toilet; I think I must have a UTI. I tinkle without light, flush and wash before drying my hands and navigating back through the dark lounge to my room, head on the pillow I fall back into dreamland.

I wake up early wanting a pie for breakfast after another pee. I stop at the bakery on my way to work and pop next door to the doctor to book an appointment. They have one there and then, so I head in.

'What's going on?' Dr Smyth asks as I plop down.

'I need to wee all the time. Probably need some Ural or such.'

'Are you drinking lots? How is your health overall? When was your last period? Are you faint at all?' He asks all sorts of irrelevant questions before sending me to do a urine test.

At lunchtime, I'm called back to see the doctor and I sit down, waiting to get my script.

'Krystal, take a seat. When was your last period?'

Back to this stupid question.

'I really don't know, I'm irregular and don't pay attention,' I repeat.

'Congratulations, you are pregnant.'

'Ha, ha, seriously can I just have the UTI treatment, please?'.

'Sorry, I need you to have a scan.'

Somehow, I leave the doctors. I don't remember paying and I don't remember walking down the path from the clinic past my work, past the bakery and into the x-ray place. I don't remember talking to the receptionist. I don't remember anything until the cool gel is lathered on my stomach and the ultrasound stick presses into my bladder where a little wriggling black-and-white creature within me waves on the screen while warm tears flow down my face.

I do remember walking back to work, finding a job to do involving minimal customer interaction, counting money, checking transactions, and watching the time go by.

Three months, my baby is three months old. It's a month since I've seen Gavin. I have to tell him. He always said he didn't want kids. I've never really cared, but all afternoon my hands protectively cup my stomach. I care now. Planned or not planned, wanted, or not wanted. Now wanted, this child is my future. I already know I'll do anything for it.

Being Wednesday night Gavin wouldn't be out and I didn't want to knock on his door, but I need to plan what to say to him so after work, I drive down to our beach—Kohimarama.

I sit running my hands through the sand, daydreaming about our future. I'm so deeply immersed in thoughts of Gavin, me, and the wriggler, that when I hear his voice, I don't realise it's real, but it is. I glance up and smile at him. He's walking towards the ocean, in the navy board shorts I'd bought him for Christmas, his abs glinting in the setting sun. My hand lifts to wave until I see his hand slip around the waist of a woman beside him. She has short dark hair. He likes long-haired fair women, like me. He'd told me. Her stomach, she's pregnant. Gavin's having a baby with somebody else as well. Has he been with her and me? Am I just the woman on the side? I can't have been—we've always had deep heart-to-hearts. He said he couldn't have a relationship while he's working away. I'd believed him.

'Guess it's just us, little one.' I rub my mini-me, then stand up to leave.

Gavin sees my tear-stained face and he lets go of her hand. I run to my car. All those pillowed moments between us have been lies. I thought I knew him better than anyone—but I was wrong.

I sit in the car and bury my face in my hands. Focused on breathing I don't see him until there's a tap on the window. I turn the car on and do the worst exit of a parallel park in the history of automobiles. I take off, narrowly missing a cyclist, and drive around Tamaki Drive and into the Kelly Tarlton's carpark. I imagine bringing my wriggler here one day, but how will I afford the admission price on my own? It's unsafe to drive while shaking so I park for half an hour until my need to wee overcomes everything else. Around a few more bends I head into KFC. Can pregnant people eat KFC? I don't care.

I do the only thing I have left to do, pull up in Mum and Dad's driveway. I can hear the screaming before I get out of the car. I leave as this is clearly not the time to share my news.

Home in my flat, I place the KFC in the fridge with a note for my flatmate saying, 'help yourself,' and I make a cheese toastie, then a second, and a third. When I can hold the phone steady enough to do a Google search, I find out what foods I can and can't eat and create the tightest budget.

Five months later.

I now live in Mum's new flat while she travels the world alone. Dad lives with his sister down the line. After gambling half their house away, he has to start afresh.

I water my potted veggie garden which is helping me live on a tiny budget, before manoeuvring into my new fuel-efficient car. I arrive just in time for my first antenatal class, where I will learn how to put a baby in and out of a car seat. Introductions start at the other end of the room thankfully. The pregnant parents talk about how they planned their babies and are baby proofing their mansions. They discuss how they can afford to save the babies' placentas and all that privileged shit that I can't do.

Introductions move to the couples in the back row, where a girl tells the story of how she and her man don't want to get married but had been trying for a child for over a year and how blessed they are to finally have their baby. And the man next to her... is my Gavin. My baby's daddy. They have been together for over a year. Well, I had been with him longer and slept in his bed many times in the last year. I know he doesn't want to get married, as his parents have such a toxic marriage. His eyes are fixed on me.

By the time it gets to me, I'm shaking. I don't know what to say. I want to say it's his baby, but I can't. In tears I managed to get out,

'My name is Krystal.' I mutter a few unintelligible words and then say, 'Thank you.' I haven't given anything away except the fact that I'm a total airhead by the end of class.

I'm the first to leave, I run to my car and again Gavin follows. This time when I pull out, I narrowly avoid hitting a bus. Driving near Gavin is clearly a skill I have not acquired.

One month later.

The birth is relatively textbook. Water breaks, slowly go into hospital, open my legs, puff, and pant, and become a mum. It's the looks on the doctors' faces as they look at my baby boy that is not textbook. He is whipped away, and I don't get to feed him. Don't get to hold him. I don't know if he has two eyes or three. If he looks like Gavin, or me. I do more of what I've been doing too much the last nine months: crying.

I'm eventually allowed to get up, and I go for a walk, I drag my feet up and down the ward overlooking the Hauraki Gulf, where people are on yachts, laughing, drinking champagne without any worries. Here I am, my flesh and blood never having been held. I look up around and see Gavin jiggling a mass of pink. I need to know—when he sees me, I ask,

'When was she born?'

'Midday today,' he replies. 'Are you okay?'

My baby's half-sister shares his birthday. She has a father and love. She is able to be cared for and carried. I slide down the wall and hug my legs, screaming a gurgling cry. Gavin tries to talk to me. I stay there and eventually Gavin comes back without the baby, but with a nurse. The nurse says she needs me back in my room. Gavin and the nurse support me to my bed. My baby is in there sleeping in an incubator. A team of doctors arrive saying my baby has heart issues and needs an operation now. They need the consent of the parents and ask who the father is. I lift my finger and point at Gavin. His finger twitches as he points to himself, and I nod.

'Why didn't you tell me?'

There are no words.

Gavin holds me as our baby is wheeled off for an operation. He hops in bed beside me, my arm around him the way we used to lay.

'I wish you'd told me,' he repeats.

I still have no words till I finally say, 'Please talk to me. Tell me what's been going on in your life, just not about her.'

He tells me all about work and cricket. Just like he used to. He talks until I fall asleep. I wake as he slides back into my bed and kisses me on the cheek. There is a bunch of flowers in a vase and some baby clothes.

Sometime later our baby comes back. We can finally hold him. The three of us cuddle on the bed and the nurse takes our first family photo. In his arms we discuss names, he wants William—a family name. I think why not, that'll be cool. I WILL be a good mum. I WILL do the best that I can for this little boy and I WILL love him till my dying breath.

I manage to avoid Gavin for the next five years, until Will's first day of school.

Walking Past a Bench on the Gulf

Jackson Lowe

Concrete and tar leaks to the brow of the beach
I'm on the move
In and out
Weaving past slower things
Decorations of old people

A walking cane
Purple earrings, a silver watch
Elderly accessories

My mouth has
A bland taste
Maybe

Behind each wrinkle
Great story, a new flavor

I'm still
Moving
The city scape across the stomach of ocean

Unacknowledged
Every step in pace with my lungs
And judgments

To a halting pause
Looking away from my destination
Amongst the seagulls
An old man (particularly old)

Perched upon a bench
His view, the gaze
Anchors my curiosity

He seems to be looking beyond, far
Much further than the city scape
I won't notice

"Excuse me Sir..."

For the first time today
I adjust to a polite posture

"I was just interested in knowing what you may be
thinking about?"

"Oh... absolutely nothing, I suppose"
My reply is natural and obvious

"Damn... I hope I can be like that - like you one day"

A smile with a chuckle

My feet took off
Falling back
Into rhythm
With my lungs and judgements of slower things

And on the trip back
I passed the same man on the same bench
And I knew
He was thinking
About absolutely nothing

Murray's Bay. Image: Susan Glamuzina

The Hauraki Gulf (G)host

Chantelle Van Vuuren

Mid-December. 7a.m. Bayswater Marina.
Me in all black. The sky, all blue. The sea, flat.
My first trip to Waiheke Island.
Strangers dressed in white linen, holding hands beneath an arch on
the beach.
Floating home on the afternoon's gentle wind, arms out, eyes
closed, twenty-one years old and happy.

30 December 2023. Radio New Zealand reports that
most Auckland beaches are facing sewage overflows and that
people shouldn't swim.
Again.

The height of summer and the Coromandel crawl.
The traffic swell along clear coast. The pilgrimage to the trip taken
with my grandparents in 2009 where we made money from paper
and joy was a car ride and a stroll along Hot Water Beach.

28 November 2023. An article from Stuff looks at an open
letter addressed to the Government, warning that, without greater
environmental protection,
the Hauraki Gulf may become an underwater graveyard.

Wednesday evening. 6:30 p.m. Viaduct Harbour.

My first time on a catamaran. A Christmas gift my mother found. A darker sky but still a cerulean expanse.

We drift beneath the Harbour Bridge, out to sea, and people dance and stumble in a weightless way but

I am haunted by the harrowing realisation that

the swims I've had, freedom felt, sights seen, are ones my own children may never know.

Twenty-one years old, arms anchored, eyes open.

Luminous. Image: Susan Glamuzina

Owls and Larks, Ribbons and Locks

Suzanne Weld

Anna sits on a park bench in the shade of a sprawling pōhutukawa. It's one of many hugging the shoreline of Mission Bay. These ancient trees provide a refuge from the constant stream of weekend traffic on Tamaki Drive. In front of her, four bikini-clad twenty-somethings sunbathe on multi-coloured beach towels, lined up on the sparkling, yellow sand. Mid-beach, a bunch of teens playing French cricket whoop as the batsman is caught out. A family near the tide scoop up water and pour it into the moat of their wonky sandcastle. Anna's eyes skim the glassy Waitematā, alight on Rangitoto, then zoom out to the other islands nestled in the haze of the Hauraki Gulf.

Her gaze blurs. It's almost one year since she and Tom first met. She'd been resting on a similar seat in Kohimarama, after walking Jasper in the late-summer sun. She'd been texting, the hot northerly buffeting her auburn hair back towards Tamaki Drive, Jasper panting on the cool grass at her feet.

Tom had just beached his kayak on the top of the tide which slapped against the damp, warm sand. He'd rolled out into the retreating waves, then dragged his craft as fast as he could over the scorching beach. As he lurched it up on to the grass, Jasper had darted towards him and when Anna felt the sudden tug of his lead, she'd jumped up, yanking him back.

"Hey, here boy! Oooh, sorry." Looking up, she saw a bedraggled Tom twisting his paddle into the bow of his kayak.

"No worries." Flicking his dripping, dark locks off his face, he threw her a wry smile and proceeded to remove the top half of his wetsuit.

"What's his name?"

"Who? Oh Jasper. Jazz. And I'm Anna." She felt her face flare.

And that's how they'd got to know each other. Tom lounging with Jazz on the grass and Anna leaning in from the park bench, their conversation flowing with ease and anticipation. An hour later, swapped numbers tapped into their mobiles, they'd agreed to meet again in the weekend for a walk to Karaka Bay.

Over the following four months, they spent many short days and long nights together and while there was an undeniable connection between them, they couldn't ignore their differences.

Tom was a night owl. Anna was a lark. She was upbeat, happy-go-lucky. He overthought everything and often became mired in melancholy. She was superstitious, loved musicals and wallowed in romcoms, while he was a realist, thought musicals were frivolous rubbish, preferring dark psychodramas and dystopian films. He would laugh off her carefree outlook on life, tease her, call her Pollyanna. She soon learnt how contained he was, how his dark moods reflected feelings that she knew he held deep. They were like yin and yang. Any discord was countered by their magnetic connection which, despite forming so quickly, was solid and true.

They had planned to travel overseas together but couldn't agree where. Tom wanted to backpack around South America, visit ancient Mayan ruins in Mexico and watch the sun rise over Machu Picchu. Anna dreamt of cruising rivers in Italy and France, exploring Paris and watching sunsets over the Cote D'Azur.

"Europe is so romantic. There are all those love lock bridges," she gushed. "The most famous is Le Pont des Arts in Paris."

"Yeah, and now it's collapsing under all the weight of those bloody locks," scoffed Tom.

Their differences kept emerging like pieces of driftwood, thrown up and strewn onto a beach after a storm. Despite brushing them aside, they couldn't deny their connection was starting to fray.

One blustery, winter Sunday, as they climbed Rangitoto, they found themselves in an explosive exchange of faltering, half sentences, cut short by icy squalls of emotion. On the ferry back to Auckland, their remaining words were so loaded with anger, they plummeted like heavy hailstones into the frigid water around them.

After a week's silence, emotions quelled but guarded, they spoke on the phone.

"I need space, more time to think about what I want," said Tom.

"Take all the time you need." Anna tried to keep her voice light, despite her heavy heart. She suspected she'd possibly never unlock the real Tom, free him from his self-imposed cell, but she was still hopeful.

"Let's aim to meet at our park bench. Where we first met. Say, on October the first." Tom suggested.

"Yes!" Anna cried, her mind in overdrive, replaying movie scenes of couples reuniting at a nominated spot after spending time apart. "If we both turn up it means we want to be together, and..."

"And if one or both of us are a no-show, we know that's it." Tom finished her sentence, blunt, to the point. "So, what time? Ten o'clock?"

"Yup, good." Anna said, inwardly beaming.

Anna knows she's early. She parks and jogs across Tamaki Drive towards Kohi beach, her high pony-tail swinging, her heart pounding out hope. Slow down, take your time. Tom's restraint thrums through her and she slows her pace. She reaches the verdant bank and its bold parade of pōhutukawa that run with the beach, east to west. Above her, tūī flit and plunge into the billowing, grape-green foliage. They seem to be cajoling each other to find the first of the plump, silvery buds about to burst into crimson brilliance. Calm, cobalt waves shush back and forth, nudging the tawny sand and retreating, nudging and retreating.

Anna finds their park bench and sits. She pulls her phone from her bag and scrolls through her texts. No new messages and it's nearly ten am. The minutes pound on. Slowly. Dragging their weight. She turns and looks back, up and down the shared path, across Tamaki Drive, scanning the footpath on the other side. She sighs and checks the shoreline in case Tom has decided to arrive like the first time they met. The tide is going out.

Five past ten. Six past. Now seven. Eight. Nine. Shoulders slumped, her heart falls in slow motion. At a quarter past, Anna's eyes blur with tears. She yanks the white ribbon from her ponytail. Her hair falls around her face like a dark veil. Distraught, her heart and mind swimming against each other, she hastily ties the ribbon to the metal arm of the seat and runs back to her car.

A white ribbon rises and falls on the cooling breeze. It's late afternoon and the wind has picked up. It teases the ribbon on the metal armrest, making it flap madly like a flag at a half-mast. A few passers-by notice it, wonder why it's there. Is it simply lost from a little girl's hair or is it tethered to the park bench for a reason, a signal, a sign? They leave it there as the ribbon seems to have a purpose, a reason for being.

Tom hesitates. He wants to see Anna. If he sees her again, he's sure he will have his answer. He'll know if they should give it another crack. He hates being up in the air like this. He just wants it over and done with. He dons his leather jacket and helmet, revs his motorbike and roars down his street to the beach.

He parks close to their spot, removes his helmet and secures it to his bike. He peers between the pōhutukawa trunks. Even in the dim light he can see the park bench is vacant. He strides towards their meeting place, sits down and looks out to the inky Hauraki horizon. The waning crescent moon cuts a shimmering swathe through the choppy harbour. The chilly breeze does little to quieten the questions running on repeat through his mind.

A white ribbon taps his black, leather jacket. With his focus on the tempestuous waves, he grabs at the ribbon and it frees itself from its knot. It's loose around his fingers for a second, but with the old self-talk taking over, he barely feels it. A sudden gust whips the ribbon from his hand and carries it rippling way down the beach where it slips into darkness.

By ten past ten, his thoughts are mocking him.

"Idiot. She's not coming. What were you thinking? She's too good for someone like you."

He stands and thrusts his hands into his jacket pockets. Feeling a hard metal object, he pulls it out. It's the padlock he sometimes uses to secure his motorbike with a big chain. He twists the key, unlocks and locks it, unlocks and locks it, remembering Anna, swooning in her typical dreamy way about the romance of the love lock bridge in Paris. He opens his lock, hooks it around the thinnest part of the armrest of their park bench and snaps it shut.

Who knows? Maybe she'll see it and know who put it there for her.

Bracing himself against the cold, he strides back to his bike. He opens the throttle and roars away from the beach.

Image: Susan Glamuzina

Okahu Bay: a Sonnet

Maris O'Rourke

I first saw Tāmaki Drive when the Oriana, en route from Hawaii, glided silently into Auckland Harbour at dawn. I first saw Tāmaki Drive when the Oriana, en route from Hawaii, glided silently into Auckland Harbour at dawn. I was already on deck as New Zealand came into view. The end of the world, the beginning of the world, recognition jolted, time shifted. I had been here before. An unfamiliar sense of belonging, like the shroud of mist over the dark, impenetrable bush, enveloped me in a cloak of home. Deep feelings of peace and well-being came over me. I'd been working in Canada and Hawaii and I was on my way to Australia, planning to only pass through New Zealand. Now I'd seen it and I knew I may go away, but I would never leave.

Much later, when I was working with Tarutaru Rankin at the Auckland College of Education, I learned the concept of tūrangawaewae—your place of standing. That was what happened to me, I had found my place of standing.

I have traversed Tamaki Drive thousands of times since then, run in Round the Bays with my children, and then grandchildren, in push-chairs, walked the beaches deep in thought while writing poetry in my head and sat en route at my favourite benches in Ōkahu Bay and Mission Bay to write up ideas in my ever-present notebook.

I've watched the erosion and rescue attempts and admired the rocky breakwaters created by the tireless local groups.

I walk regularly from home in Mt Eden around the waterfront to St Heliers – it's my favourite walk in Auckland.

Inspired by the history, events and environment, I wrote the poem below:

Below Bastion Point, a sweet sweeping
of flowering Pōhutukawa trees,
holds grassy slopes just right for sleeping;
dreaming of wrongs no-one can appease.

Where Ngāti Whātua once gathered kai
on tidal flats tourists paddle in the heat.
Middens where sewer pipes now lie;
prolific shellfish beds no-one can eat.

Sheltered by the curving bluestone wall,
where the tide eats up the bay twice a day,
old people watch slow ripples rise and fall -
inexorable forces no-one can stay.

In the playground, children scream and twist
by tūpuna no-one can now evict.

Okahu Bay. Image: Denise T O'Hagan

Notes on the Botany
of Shakespear, Whangaparāoa Peninsula

Marley Ford

When one thinks of the botany of the Whangaparāoa Peninsula it is hard not to think of the past. A few pōhutukawa (*Metrosideros excelsa*) cling to the coastal cliff, seldom noticed until their summer jubilee, telling a story of human arrival and a landscape greatly modified. Historically, the soil is rich from seabirds, with a thick cloak of coastal forest. The vegetation has been reduced to thin dry pasture, forest fragments and isolated individuals clinging to cliffs. However, an attempt at refugium has been made, a fence to stop predators and an effort to reforest the headland. Here, a collection of lesser-known plants and grasses from Shakespear Park are used to share the history of the Peninsula's past and give links to other places from the perspective of a botanist.

Shakespear Regional Park is located at the Eastern tip of the Whangaparāoa Peninsula. The park is named after the family who purchased the farm from local iwi, Ngāti Kahu, in the 1880s. They later sold the land to the Auckland Regional Council (Auckland Regional Council, 1991). Shakespear has a deep history of human occupation, stretching back one thousand years (Auckland Regional Council, 1991). The northern area of the park was acquired by the New Zealand Army during World War II (Cameron et al., 2008). A 1.7 km predator-proof fence across the peninsula was completed in 2011 (Bracewell-Worrall, 2016).

Grasses are greatly important to the human story, from the

economic importance of wheat (*Triticum aestivum*), corn (*Zea mays*) and rice (*Oryza sativa*), pasture for livestock to the role in human ritual (scented holy grass, *Anthoxanthum* spp.). Our native New Zealand grass flora is diverse but often forgotten when thinking of clean, green New Zealand. The line between native and exotic is often blurry - some species have been weeds here longer than others. Some are widespread and some extremely localised. Dry grasslands are an uncommon vegetation association in the north, with plenty of historic interest in their species composition. Grasses are used here to study our relationship to the land.

The lush coastal forest of Auckland has been burnt and cleared since human arrival, giving the chance for grasses to thrive in coastal Auckland. Once thought an exotic, the native paspalum, sometimes called taranui (*Paspalum orbiculare*, Figure 1) forms an Auckland stronghold in the Army lands of Shakespear Park. This species is linked to Polynesia; it is common in the wider Pacific and Australia. Taranui is a species of marginal land, the low coastal scrub offers a refugium for this 'Threatened – Nationally Vulnerable' species (Simpkins et al., 2022) to persist while similar local habitats have been developed. The paspalum grows in gumland-like scrub with *Pentapogon rarus*, thought of as an early introduction from Australia. The relatively undisturbed military training grounds give refuge to the native grasses and the earlier arrivals. This could be from a lack of visitors or the absence of modification by dogs, blackbirds, etc. These scrub communities are prone to fire; however, this could benefit taranui, setting back the clock of succession that would eventually displace the grass unless some marginal land persisted.

Figure 1. Seedhead of the native paspalum (Paspalum orbiculare).
All photos taken by the author.

Northern New Zealand paddocks are so often dominated by grass monocultures. However, the dry grass slopes of Shakespear Park host a diversity of native and Australian species (Figure 2). These species illustrate our links to the nearby continent. The grassland habitats have the potential to provide more biodiversity value than a monoculture of rye (*Lolium* spp.) or kikuyu (*Cenchrus clandestinus*). Most common are the Australian species *Anthosachne scabra*, *Bothriochloa macra* and *Rytidosperma penicillatum*, the natives also found in Australia, *Pentapogon crinitus*, *Pentapogon micranthus* and the New Zealand endemic *Rytidosperma biannulare*. These species are common in the dry ungrazed grasslands along army fences and are maintained by mowing. Less native and diverse dry slopes support perennial ryegrass (*Lolium perenne*) and crested dog's-tail (*Cynosurus cristatus*). Native grasslands are seldom recognised in northern New Zealand. These habitats have the potential to be resilient to the hot summers of climate change. Further, the early introductions and older natives suggest recent links to Australia from grass seed and livestock.

Figure 2. Dry grassed slopes of Shakespear dominated by Australian species

Not a grass, the rush, *Juncus imbricatus* var. *chamissonis* (Figure 3) was previously unrecorded on the Peninsula. It is a rather localised weed in New Zealand (Wilcox, 2013), first recorded at Shakespear on the 12 December 2023 by the author. This plant was well established in the pasture with other rushes both native (*J. australis*) and exotic (*J. effusus*). This plant originates from South America, and it is known from Cornwall Park, Central Auckland (Wilcox, 2013) in similar sheep grazed pasture. How this plant arrived in New Zealand is unknown, but possibilities include pasture seed brought into New Zealand from other countries or seed contaminates carried on livestock. Localised weed infestations like this link to the randomness and chance of colonisation, as well as the uncertainties around arrivals. As the exotic *Juncus* will grow to dominate these communities, it shows the change in environment and the stresses older types of grassland are continually exposed to.

Figure 3. The rush Juncus imbricatus var. chamissonis in pasture.

Like the pōhutukawa clinging to the Whangaparāoa sandstone, the native blue grass *Anthosachne kingiana* ssp. *multiflora* persists (Figure 4). This blue grass is on the decline throughout the country from habitat loss and weed competition. The easily eroding cliffs provide habitat, the disturbance allowing this locally rare native to continue with little competition from weeds, perched on coastal cliffs falling into the sea. Isolation and the dynamic habitat protect these coastal cliffs from nearby seed sources of the invasive Pampas grass (*Cortaderia* sp.). Biodiversity relicts are often thought of as forests in northern New Zealand but can exist as small populations of native grasses hanging to cliffs. The relicts remind us of the destruction coastal Auckland has faced. As this continues and land use and management changes, our native plant communities need to continue to adapt or disappear. They are given time and hope with refugia like the predator proof fence of Shakespear Park.

Figure 4. The native blue grass, Anthosachne kingiana ssp. multiflora on coastal cliffs.

Grasses have played a crucial role in the story of humans and are ingrained in our history. At Shakespear Park, relicts can be seen older than humans. Habitats have changed from Polynesian time, colonialisation, urban development and now predator protection. Natural communities' structure and function have changed drastically. From extensive coastal forest, we now see dry slopes support a unique diversity of native grasses, and pastures of interesting weeds. The many aspects of grass occurrences and communities reflect the layers of human's relationship with the land. Grasses provide a glimpse into an Auckland of the past, making us think what the future will bring to our urban biodiversity, and what it will look like in the face of climate change.

Acknowledgement: I would like to thank Rhys Gardner for commenting on the draft.

References

Auckland Regional Council (1991). *Shakespear Regional Park Management plan: Archaeology and History of Human Occupation.* 31-40

Bracewell-Worrall, A. (2016, March 10). *North Island robins' big trip across the harbour.* NewsHub.

Cameron, E. K., Hayward, B. W., & Murdoch, G. J. (2008). *A Field Guide to Auckland: Exploring the region's natural and historic heritage.* Godwit.

Simpkins, E., Woolley, J., de Lange, P., Kilgour, C., Cameron, E. K., & Melzer, S. (2022). *Conservation status of vascular plant species in Tāmaki Makaurau/Auckland.* Auckland Council.

Wilcox, M. (2013). *Juncus imbricatus*: a tenacious South American rush infesting pastures in Cornwall Park and One Tree Hill Domain, Auckland. *Auckland Journal of Botany 68:1.* 97 - 98.

Round The Bays

Juliet Yates

Every year they come. Thousands determined to run along the waterfront for Round the Bays. Runners travel from all over the city—by car, bus, ferries or by cycle for the popular *fun run* of 8.4 km from Quay St in the central city to Vellenoweth Green, St Heliers.

There were over 27,000 participants in 2024.

Residents in nearby streets are warned of road closures on set-up days, during the event and on clean-up days. Local businesses have limited access during the advertised road closures. Portable toilets are installed and may remain for two days to minimise disruption. Plastic cups will be removed along the route as the last contestant reaches a water station.

Teams, organised by businesses, sport t-shirts with sponsors' emblems, logos or exotic designs. Speed fanatics, determined to be first to cross the start line, leave the majority far behind. Single runners training for long distance marathons, children, teens and older persons, some in wheel-chairs, some visually impaired with helpers, and families running with small children or baby buggies.

Gasping in the humid March heat, grasping water bottles, along Tāmaki Drive they run, past the string of beaches described in the publicity as jewels on a necklace. Past alluring, sparkling water. Temptation. Looking towards Rangitoto, waves rippling, promising a rebirth of coolness if you only just dive in.

But first they must stagger across the finishing line.

Then, laughter. Relief. They straggle over the road to the beach. Plunge into the warm sea, its temperature raised by hundreds of bodies. Refreshed, they look for their team's meeting place. The beer tent? Corporate marquees and bubbles at Madills Farm? Or sponsors' marquees set up on the Green?

Mouth of the Whau. Acrylic on canvas. Susan Glamuzina

She/Her – My Hauraki

Caroline Carlyle

She is magnificent,
though not generically so.
She is wonderous,
with gentle *wahine* wiles.
She embraces stunning beaches,
capturing everyday moments,
whilst coquettishly dancing across white sands,
dawn, noon, and evening.

Her energy is youthful, playful, and eager,
as early sunbeams glance across
her flat silky form.
Moana's silver saturation
so sensuous and dazzling,
she flirts with her islands and inlets,
slowly excavating jagged edges
and keeping *kai moana* protected in her belly.

At noon, in her prime,
she is confident and sassy,
looking for an innocent menace.
Whitecaps tease,
so haughty, mischievous,
daring and adventurous,
as she seductively encourages
a blissful nor'easterly caress.

As eastern skies turn in,
and the canvas is lit,
a unique amber glow bathes her.
She adorns a gloriously gilded gown,
most decadently audacious.
Ruahine, her marvellous maturity
and gallant graciousness,
she's now at ease, selflessly satisfied.

Hauraki Gulf Fibre Art. Caroline Carlyle

On a Cold Day in Auckland on the Edge of the Gulf

Christopher Reed

on a cold day in Auckland, on the edge of the Gulf,
beyond the veined networks of roads, tunnels, industry, the blossomed
roses from the gardens on the hill - their colours filling
the ever-moving air, the rusted foundations, the dusty tracks
empty of movement, the whomp whomp of the rescue chopper
curls itself into maternal rest.

from here the ocean, water-colouring the morning with
rippled sunlit blankets, laps the shore,
rubbing its belly on the fine sand. silent and sure. from here the city
sleeps, hunkered down in shadow and soul, an anxious weary
eventual sleep knowing little of tomorrow but carrying

scars
from its predictable past.
i see the sharp notes of muted jazz
louvered into flat stones edging the moana,
furrowing through rivulets bubbling with energy,
the home of kina, of oyster, of mussel,
the rainbow'd snap of the king, the milky fleshed fish,
pungent
and prized (a funny thought, considering), layered
thick
upon themselves.

all these things standing still,
waiting, pronounced like a pouncing cat,
what comes next, O Gulf?

whānau ano te whenua
give birth to the world once again

Golden Hour. Image: Melissa Gunn

Hauraki Lament, or a Song of Love?

Melissa Gunn

The ferry that carries us is old and slow, chugging faithfully from one jewel in the crown of the Hauraki Gulf, Tīkapa Moana, to the next. Salt crusts the edges of the windows and accumulates on the handrails. A fast commuter boat carrying tourists to Waiheke speeds past us and we wallow as its wake hits. Someone new to the sea exclaims in fear and surprise as the boat rocks from side to side. Regular sea-goers sway with the motion or grip handholds, but otherwise ignore it. The skipper, perched high up in the wheelhouse, the door open behind her so we can see. She eases the wheel round, gently guiding the old boat into a safer course.

The larger vessel recedes into the grey distance before we settle into a slower up and down motion once more. We turn away from the route the fast ferry took, sliding into the rougher waters of the channel between Rangitoto, towering Lord of the Gulf, and the crescent-shaped picnic bay of Te Motu-a-Ihenga. We're headed further on, further out into the wide wings of the Hauraki, drawn by the possibility of dolphins.

The wind rises as we navigate the channel; larger waves crash foaming across our bow and the keen-eyed observers on deck hustle inside, wiping salt spray from their expensive lenses. They linger in the aisles, balancing on loafer-clad feet, loath to admit weakness and sit. My oldest tries to emulate their insouciance, showing off to his cousins, standing between the seats. We hit an especially large wave and he staggers. I grab his shirt as he lurches past, slowing his trajectory just enough that he doesn't fall. Still trying to be cool, he jerks his chin up in acknowledgement, as if to say 'Thanks Mum,' without the embarrassment of saying it aloud.

When we reach the wider waters beyond the channel, the waves subside into a regular swell. The lens-carriers head outside again, eager to capture any signs of life on their cameras. My own camera is ready, heavy around my neck, but family duties keep me inside the ferry for now.

The skipper is looking for life too; the active wings of gannets or shearwaters fluttering above a work-up is often the only way to find dolphins in this once-teeming Gulf. Right now, the water stretches grey and empty as far as the eye can see. It's hard to believe that something so huge, so vital, could be ailing. But the evidence is all around us, in the barren emptiness of the sea and the resounding silence from the Noises as we pass rock stacks and islands that should echo with the cries of nesting seabirds.

Through the forward window, I see the ambitious lens-carriers lower their cameras in defeat. There's nothing to photograph. We continue our tour of the Hauraki, all eyes searching. We're somewhere between hope and defeat.

As we get further from the city, I begin to imagine flickers of life. Surely, that was a wing? Or the puff of air from the nasal passages of a Bryde's whale? Or even the tall black fin of an orca, slicing through the water. Every time I lift my binoculars to check, there's nothing to see but a wave or a rock. Grey sky, grey sea.

The kids are getting fractious. They were promised dolphins, or at least birds, and so far they've seen nothing but sea and sky. A quarrel begins between them, some inane bickering about who got the best sandwich. Sea and sky don't rate with this audience. I break out carefully hoarded chocolate bars in an attempt to gain harmony, and silence reigns for a few moments.

We're sweeping the coastline of Hauturu-o-Toi, Little Barrier, resting post of the winds, when at last the cry goes up. I raise my eyes from their contemplation of the sandpapered-smooth, yet salt-encrusted window sill. At last! A gannet is circling high in the sky. A lens-carrier leans forward, eager, pointing like the best of hunting dogs. There's a flurry of wings. Storm petrels—once thought extinct, but rediscovered on a trip like this one—flutter near the surface alongside their larger cousins, the black petrels. My emotions flurry too.

"Come on, kids, this is it," I say, urging them outside. My desire not to miss anything is as strong as theirs.

As we emerge onto the windy deck and compete for a position near the railing, the gannet folds its wings and plunges, entering the sea with a splash before emerging with an ungainly flap. There's nothing in its beak - it missed this time. But more gannets are moving in, soaring on the wind before making dives of their own. The petrels work in a churn of water, white against the greyness. Salt-laden wind deposits a sticky layer on our skin as we gaze in hope.

"There!" my youngest cries out. "Mum, look, a dolphin!" The sun, absent till now, emerges from the grey clouds and glints off the glassy blue-green sea. I shade my eyes to see better in this transformed world.

Everyone looks, surging over to our side of the boat, and for a moment I'm more concerned about keeping my kids from being pushed overboard than seeing dolphins. I grab at the collar of my youngest, who is too close to the edge and who surely cannot swim well enough for a fall into the sea out here. We've got a front-row seat, but the press of bodies behind us is pushing us against—and through—the railing.

My youngest slips forward, my hold on her t-shirt nearly broken by her sudden weight as she slips. I have a sudden vision of the empty depths that lie below us. Or no, not empty—there are fish, and probably sharks too. My fingers tighten on my child's clothing and I haul her back with a strength I didn't realise I possessed. She presses against me, shivering with the near miss, but her eyes still firmly on the sleek mammals we've come to see. There's a lump in my stomach, cold and hard, as I think of what nearly happened just now.

"Give us some room," I growl at the crowd, my fear coming out as anger.

Luckily, the skipper and her first mate take charge, directing people to spread out: no need to panic, everyone will get a chance to see, this is a big pod. The crowd around us eases, and as I slowly relax I see they're right. Ahead of our slowing boat, a multitude of graceful fins part the now-calm sea. There's a collective gasp as a dolphin surges forward and leaps from the water, re-entering with barely a splash. Then there's another, and another. Grey and white like the sea, but so alive. Cousins, brothers, sisters, uncles and aunts, no doubt, all travelling together. I barely remember to raise my camera. My heart is too full of joy at the sight of these small cetaceans.

"Look, Mum, there's a baby," my oldest points out, more restrained than my youngest, but with a tone full of awe. "Can you get a photo?"

I recall that these dolphins are studied, and someone might well be able to identify the individuals from their unique fin and scar marks, so I photograph every dolphin in sight after all, click after click.

"The baby's in trouble," my youngest says. "Look, it's getting too close to the boat."

The crowd around us gives a collective gasp as everyone sees what's happening. As the dolphins surge through the water, taking turns to leap just ahead of our bow, the dolphin calf is doing the same. But it's slower than its pod-mates, perhaps not strong enough for such speed yet. Any moment, the hard edge of the bow is going to hit the little dolphin. The same fear I felt for my own child manifests in my stomach as I watch this other mother's baby slip into danger.

"Turn the boat," my youngest yells. "Look out!"

There's a moment of collective tension. Everyone's eyes are on the dolphin as the skipper spins the wheel hard. Perhaps she throws the boat's engines into reverse, too. There's certainly an enormous graunching noise from below. The deck tilts from the speed of our turn, but we're still moving forwards. The boat slips closer, closer to the dolphin calf. At the last possible second, there's a flurry of movement in the water. An adult dolphin soars through the water, tail flapping furiously, heading straight for the calf. It angles its body so that it hits it from the side, nudging it out of the way of our boat. Then, it twists itself away, leaping through the air before arrowing ahead with the calf at its side, miraculously unharmed.

There's a joint sigh of relief before, predictably, the clicking of cameras resumes. The skipper keeps the boat stationary until the pod tires of playing around our boat and heads off into the distance.

The trip home is shorter than the outward leg; no need to search now. The skipper is being kind to her boat, not pushing her so hard on our return journey. The patch of rough sea in the channel barely raises a squeak. The kids are quiet too, either tired, or thinking, as I am.

The joy of seeing dolphins used to be a common from the shore or from small boats. Not something that had to be sought out at great expense. Somehow, we've laid waste to the treasures of this place, and only a few sparkles remain. I think of the baby dolphin. *We'll take care of you,* I think. *You and your mum, and your cousins too.* My kids aren't the only ones who need someone to look out for them.

Dolphins. Image: Melissa Gunn

Out of Reach

S A Thomas

it's early morning and I'm at your beach
the one we went to a quarter of a century ago
together hand-in-hand
you'd introduce me to your parents
I miss your parents so much
I don't remember where we sat
or which roads we walked
I do remember being close
listening to your wonderful stories
I wish we could be together again here
we can't sit here and have a picnic
we'll never complain about the dogs
or laugh at the person who fell over
no sharing strawberries anymore
if we could, we would reminisce
looking over at Rangitoto
she looks so close
close enough to swim to – but she's not

we both enjoy swimming
we don't swim together
we don't do anything together

that's the way it has to be
it's the way it needs to be
it's not the way I want it to be
I dream of snuggling in your thrumming chest
making music with the rolling waves
just like Rangitoto
you're out of reach
out of reach
gone

Rain Affair

S A Thomas

Escaped on the Fly

Denise T O'Hagan

Tikitiboo bounced along in the open harbour. A day trip to Motuihe Island. Son and husband stood at the helm of our little four-metre gad-about that had belonged to my dad. The girls and I squished together on the white foam cushions at the back. Sun streamed down through blue sky sprinkled with candyfloss clouds, while the horizontal wind made Medusas of us, our snake-like locks reaching out towards Sky Tower and the city behind.

The orange blow-up rubber dinghy we used as a biscuit filled the bottom of the boat. My jaw clenched. 'Fun and games' ahead, an activity I dreaded but endured as the kids gripped with blue-knuckled reins and flew over open sea on the unstable bouncy castle trailing behind the speeding boat.

'Safe as houses. What are you talking about?' My husband said, as the kids nodded in eager agreement. I put my overprotectiveness in my pocket, and hid my anxiety with a smile.

As Rangitoto roared past port side and Browns Island/Motukorea sailed away on our right, our destination approached up ahead. The boat swerved imperceptibly sideways and the boys swivelled around in unison to peer at us, a secret look between them, then turned back to steering the boat.

We beached the craft ocean-side at Takutairaroa Bay and jumped out. My husband nonchalantly commented that he didn't think we'd go biscuiting today, a bit too windy and choppy. My son agreed. My breath escaped, my shoulders relaxed.

'Ok, sure,' I said, nodding and trying not to sound too pleased. We unloaded our supplies of towels, sunscreen, water, bacon and egg pie, chips and cherries and settled on the beach for a picnic.

After lunch and a swim, we went for a walk to the top of the hill. Graves of scarlet fever and influenza victims provided a sad reminder of Auckland's Quarantine Station, set up here from 1872. Windswept views of the Hauraki Gulf dominating from the clifftops, a reminder of how the settlers' arduous journey had ended in full view of the mainland.

We wandered back along the dusty gravel track, crickets and grasshoppers singing amongst the tall grasses to the chorus of sunshine. Sheltered under the pines on the quiet leeward side of the island, we ate well-deserved ice blocks from a caravan shop. Boaties waded knee deep out into the harbour from Waihaorangatahi Bay. The tide had gone out so far that their boats would be marooned for hours. Grateful to have anchored at Ocean Beach, we clambered aboard Tikitiboo, manoeuvring around the unused blow-up dinghy in the bottom of the boat and headed home, sun-bleached, salty and satisfied.

The truth spilled over fish and chips out of earshot of little ears that night. My husband and son had seen a two-metre shark, jaws wide open, soaring airborne in front of the boat as we'd approached the island. Our biscuiting adventure had been canned in fact by the creatures of the deep.

Out on the Harbour. Image: Denise T O'Hagan

Overboard

Lee Simpson

The most common person to commit murder is the spouse, as murders are generally caused by passion. So, as I look at my newly renovated kitchen, the white tiles pooled with red, I wonder how I will not get blamed for his murder. I scoop up his phone. I remember reading how police use phone tracking to solve homicides—I have to be smart.

I drive my car and my phone to my friend's house. She's away and I'm feeding her cat, Gingerbear. The cat weaves between my legs as I pace trying to come up with a plan. I leave my phone and car there and, in her black clothes and hat, I bus the seven blocks home.

Now what to do. I unlock his phone and look for anything. No dodgy photos. No weird messages. No porn. Then I find a recently deleted message folder.

Sex photos, his dick pic makes me want to hurl—his mole is so off putting. Gross! The asshole is cheating on me, now it's really going to look like it was me who killed the son-of-a-bitch. *Think, think, think.* I message her, whoever she is, and say '*I need to meet*'.

In the laundry I open black rubbish sacks with gloves on. The room is small and it's reasonably easy to quickly tape up all the surfaces with the slippery bags. I wear a black bag too; it would almost look comical—if not for all the blood. But hey, I'm a nurse, I can do blood. Then I find his newest expensive tool, which my wages paid for. I think back to every crime show I've ever watched and avoiding the joints I make his body small enough to fit into four bags. I put all the bags in with the body, my rubbish sack dress and bricks for weights.

The bags are loaded into the back of his boot with the golf bag we couldn't afford. I return to the scene and check his phone. The slut has messaged back.

I see his sandwich on the plate. All he had to do was pick the cucumber out and be grateful—he would still be alive. Every man should know not to complain about the food a woman's made him while she still holds the knife. Especially this time of the month!

With the bags and phone in his stupid Land Rover, I drive to the boat ramp on the Hauraki Gulf. A beautiful day. I find a random rowboat and some oars and load the four bags in the boat. I can't believe no one is around—what a dodgy little spot. I wonder if he met his slag friend here for hook ups. I row him out and dump the bags overboard in four different spots and row back in. No spilt blood and if there are security cameras, I am confident I don't look like me in Jane's clothes.

As a car pulls up, from the shadows of some pine trees I message the slut from his phone, 'I have decided to do the right thing by my wife, she loves me and I'm going to give her my all.'

I see a lady get out of a yellow Toyota and walk to my Hubby's car. I don't know her at all but as she looks for him, I slip his phone in under her seat and melt into the trees again. Jane's place is an easy walk from the secluded bay, so I walk back to her place where I have the best shower of my life. I wash her clothes and shower with the strongest bleach I can find before I return to the landrover and slowly drive home. Once my house is as blood free as Jane's I wait, watching romantic movies till midnight, then I start making the panicked calls, the calls that will get the cheater in jail—or if I screwed up, me.

The waiting game begins!

Ocean Lava

Angela Vuletich

49 Summers

Amanda Eason

She carries her lanky 7-year-old through the bright starred night,
along the sharp path to the dunny. One child settles and the other
starts up. It's hard, she says, at the kitchen sink.

Reflected in the eyes of grey-haired bach holders, Paul walked here
49 summers. His wedding guests on The Green, they painted his bach
(no. 19) safe white as he wasted across the Waitematā.

Now bach 34's grandad asks about another ceremony.
But Rachel, who knows she must, in time, remove her glittering bands—
isn't ready ... When his ashes are scattered here

on the cold, black lava of this young volcano—his dry
calcium phosphates
and salts of sodium and potassium will sift into airy
scoria pockets
to be found by greedy pōhutukawa roots.

He will rise up, through the trunks and branches and
twigs
of the Rangitoto trees he loved, til bursting forth—a
fiery froth of red.

In memory of Paul Sharp (23.10.1962 – 29.4.2011)

Bach 19. Image: Rachel Sharp

Auckland Naturalists' Field Club – 1882

Jenny Clay

She rearranged her hat. Ellen followed her brother over the basalt and lava. There was little shelter apart from her hat. Her drawing materials were in the bag on her shoulder.

The group of about thirty had caught the steamer to Rangitoto. It was only a half hour run. The climb was something else.

Some of the men tied their trousers with flax, others found stout pieces of wood like alpenstocks. Coats and jackets were left in a pile on the beach. Some stayed at the bottom, fishing, or by the lagoon.

Thomas led their group up the old lava streams, over boulders of scoria. Patches of coarse grass only disguised cavities legs could slip into. He pointed at the low-lying mountain mosses. She did a sketch, noting the colours, and he removed small samples.

Before the ascent there was low bush. From then on the main view was black and lichen coloured lava, with only the odd pōhutukawa, dwarf rātā, koromiko, and clusters of flax. It was already getting hot.

'Hurry up,' her brother called. He was striding ahead.

Clara, her sister, climbed beside her. Their friends were much further behind. Ellen slipped slightly, her gown catching on the edge of something sharp.

'Give her a hand Robert.'

It was Clara who released it from the rock. They continued

together.

How did Thomas expect them to keep up? His legs were much longer than theirs.

'Can you draw this one?' He'd found another specimen.

Sweat was seeping into her clothes. The sun beating against the black boulders made the heat more intense. Her mouth was dry. Talking had all but ceased among the hikers. Thomas passed around some leaves of the koromiko.

'It helps to produce saliva,' he said.

There were noises up ahead. Some young men, who had made the climb before, were coming back down, making it look easy. It wasn't.

Halfway up, the group shared much of the water that was carried.

From the base of the cone there was the final scramble. Ellen began to pitch forward and grabbed a fern. It came away in her hand. Clara helped her up. The group followed a zig-zag pattern. Only a dozen reached the cone.

They sat and rested at the top. The view across the Hauraki Gulf was spectacular: to the Waitakere Ranges to the west, over Auckland town, towards the Tangihua Ranges in the north, and to the east the Coromandel Ranges.

Thomas was picking up small pieces of rock.

The afternoon was getting late. The trip down was easier, and quicker. At the bottom some bathed in the lagoon. Emma dipped her sore feet.

'Watch out for sting-rays. Sharks,' a journalist called out.

On the steamer everyone rushed for the fresh water supply, with any vessel, including a cake tin. Ellen looked at the tears in her skirt. She flicked through her sketches. Thomas would be pleased with the record and the samples for the museum.

Early Sightings

Jenny Clay

Mixed media

Black Rock Reef

Anni Docking

(Ode to Wordsworth)

Bobbing out beyond the old yellow buoy,
thoughts wander like kites. Dancing above bright sands,
'lonely as a cloud'
snagging the obsidian reef where once – remember? –
we discovered an orphaned baby seal...

Skipping like unravelling string, thoughts flitting across miles of
emerald sea.
Slipping knots, like the years sliding out between us,
mind's eye wandering...
sprightly red & white stripes of a moody lighthouse,
flirting around the barnacled skirts of Rangitoto Island –
dipping over sacred isle Motutapu, Firth of Thames beyond –
waltzing across mussel-bound flats of Te Kōuma Harbour
curving incessantly towards Coromandel...
dallying there with wayward ghosts of miners.
Skeletal frames
still copper-panning riverbeds for flecks of gold in the gloaming.
Meandering through Manaia Valley,
crossing over that threadbare single-lane bridge...

Once,
a herd of wild horses emerged from the river-mist and cantered into
headlights,
surrounding our car with thunder and fright, before
charging into the moonlit midnight, disappearing into the hills
leaving just a silhouette.
Wooden church with the shaky lopsided frame, abandoned,
crooked windows a legacy of the last cyclone...

Kite floats on tiptoes now, buffeted by north-west winds...
tail ribbons fluttering, flicking above clasped hands,
the rising chest of an overlord:
Hauraki Gulf.
Cradled beneath a shallow moon,
I listen as Ranginui, Sky Father, speaks...
'Shhhh, don't wake him!'...
Floating Island.
Castle Rock, *Motutere,* the Sleeping Giant.

I dream...

* * *

Tracing a stolen memory of your face
– on that unexpected night –
acute vision of eyes on mine, iris edges brimming with hazel flecks
and
– there! –
startling specks of ocean-blue, a shimmer of ochre,
amusement crinkling the corners of your mouth...
So perfectly still we stood...
– moments lost –

oneness mingling with otherness.
Minutes unseen – your gaze never leaving my face –
until '*Come!*'
...we race through the lobby as the film begins...

Later, our voices trace evening shadows sloping and slinking
themselves around street corners...
From viewing *The Artist,* discussing this dichotomy of
screen and stage, we stumble our warm bodies, close-wrapped,
through the half-open door as the waiter nods...
wedging ourselves into the corner window-table,
Italian pizzeria, last customers –

Lucky fate!
Serendipitous haven.
Sweet shelter from the sodden slow midnight air.
Heaven is a shared wine glass...
– a toast –
to life's rewards, to each, to other,
spirits blooming to possibilities. Jane Eyre and her Rochester...
You suddenly ask: 'Do I believe in marriage?'
Oh!
A debate ensues.
The vagaries of courtship – if only it were possible!
A wish for this world tonight to remain perfectly still, contained in a
book,
pressed between pages like dried flowers,
this aroma of love preserved for
eternity.

* * *

In slight winds,
my errant kite descends to fade upon the twilight,
accompanied by swell and surge of interminable ocean,
scoria mixing with saltwater molecules, flotsam,
spiky seagrass, calcite shells...
– tide receding –

Memories embraced by Papatūānuku, Earth Mother,
a verdigris crowd upon a burnt beach.

Black Rock Reef in solitude,
hosting a dance
of daffodils.

Black Rock Reef. Image: A. Docking

Up the Boohai

Karen Morris-Denby

A Short Script to be adapted for Film

Sequel to 'Down Under Dominion Road' first published in 'Tales from Dominion Road' 2023

N.B. Boohai: Kiwi slang meaning isolated place.
Conchie: Shortened terminology for Conscientious Objector.
Bach: Small New Zealand holiday cottage.
Digger: A term of endearment for Australian and New Zealand soldiers.

FADE IN:
EXTERIOR:
GREAT BARRIER ISLAND 1956 – MID MORNING

Sisters *ARTY* aged 22 and *COOKY* aged 20 scramble along a bush track. *ARTY* carries a picnic basket. *COOKY* uses a folded sun umbrella as a walking stick.
ARTY

Hurry up.

COOKY

I'm getting tired. I'm sick of walking.

ARTY

Look!

ARTY points into the distance. A small bach in disrepair is partially hidden in the trees.

INTERIOR: BACH A SMALL UNKEPT KITCHEN—MID MORNING
ARTY and *COOKY* set up food on a small table. The sun umbrella leans against the table.

COOKY

Do you think anyone stays here?

ARTY

It's hard to say.

2. EXTERIOR:
BUSHLAND GREAT BARRIER ISLAND - MID MORNING
ARCH a rugged man in his 40's wears the typical classic Great Barrier Island outdoor man 'uniform'. Shorts, merino singlet over a t-shirt and standard issue gumboots. *MARK* in his late 20's, walks with *ARCH* along a bush track. They carry fishing rods and wet sugar

sacks filled with fish. *VIOLA* 12 years of age walks behind them. She carries a small empty sack. *VIOLA* is deaf. *ARCH* and *VIOLA* have their own sign language to communicate.

MARK

You can come back to the mainland Uncle Arch.

ARCH

No. I can't. What would happen to Viola? How do you think she would manage?

MARK

It's about time she met up with kids her own age.

Nobody will know you are a conchie.

ARCH

The old Diggers never forget. Anyway, nobody would give me a job.

MARK

Think of the girl. Are you going to keep her hidden forever?

Has she been with other kids? Other girls? Women to tell her...

ARCH

Before Millie got sick, she took Viola to Auckland. She was very protective. I doubt if she met other kids.

MARK

So, since her Mum died, she hasn't been with other females?

ARCH

Not really.

MARK

Who is she going to talk... girl things with?

ARCH

I gave her all the books you gave me about all that business.

MARK

Uncle Arch. We don't know about all that stuff.

She needs to talk to a... woman.

3. INTERIOR: BACH - MID MORNING
COOKY and *ARTY* look out the window. They see *ARCH MARK* and *VIOLA* walking towards the bach.
COOKY

What shall we do?

ARTY

Just be cool. We'll explain.

COOKY picks up the umbrella and makes a stance as though she will use the umbrella as a weapon.

4. EXTERIOR: BACH—MID MORNING
ARCH and *MARK* clean and gut fish.
ARCH

Don't look now but I have uninvited guests.

INTERIOR: BACH - MID MORNING
ARCH MARK and *VIOLA* stand in the doorway.

ARTY

I'm sorry, we thought this bach was abandoned.

COOKY stands pointing the umbrella at *ARCH. ARTY* starts packing up the food.

ARCH

I think we have a situation.

MARK

They might keep their mouths shut.

ARTY

Oh yes, we can keep our mouths shut.

COOKY

Maybe we can't. Who are you? Wanted murderers?

Thieves with a young girl you kidnapped.

ARTY

Wait, wait, we know you... Arch Baldwin?

COOKY

Of course. I remember. You rescued us from a flooded drain.

MARK

What are you talking about?

COOKY

We helped you escape from the police.

MARK

What's this all about?

ARCH

When I was hiding in the drain during the war, these girls, much younger then, helped me to run from the police. I would have been arrested for being a conchie if it wasn't for them.

MARK

You have never told me about that.

ARCH

Let sleeping dogs...

MARK

OK.

5. INTERIOR: BACH—LATE AFTERNOON
ARTY, VIOLA and *ARCH* sit at the kitchen table. *MARK* and *COOKY* make tea.
They are obviously attracted to each other. *ARCH* looks over to *MARK* and *COOKY*.

ARCH

Hey you two. Don't get too chummy.

COOKY

What do you mean?

ARCH

I can see you two have googly eyes for each other.

MARK

Well, you must admit she is a looker.

ARTY

Hands off my sister matey.

MARK

I'm a perfect gentleman.

MARK bows ceremoniously. *ARCH* signs and speaks to *VIOLA*.
ARCH

Love birds.

VIOLA signs to *ARCH*.
VIOLA

Kissy kissy.

ARCH and *VIOLA* laugh.
ARTY

I have just had an idea. We can take Viola. We'll look after her. Get her into a special school for deaf kids. We would come back on the weekends.

VIOLA signs to *ARCH*.
VIOLA

What did she say?

6. *ARCH* signs and speaks to *VIOLA*.
ARCH

Arty will take you to a special school. Get up to speed with lessons. You live with her and Cooky through the week then come home on the weekends.

VIOLA is upset. She storms out pushing past *ARTY*

ARTY

I didn't want to make her unhappy.

We have to go now. Can we come back soon?

ARCH

I don't know.

ARTY

Those two love birds will be hanging around together.

ARTY and *ARCH* laugh.
ARTY

I hope Viola understands we want to help.

We will love her you know.

EXTERIOR: 1958 AUCKLAND SUBURBIA-DAY
INTERIOR: KITCHEN—MORNING
ARTY sits at the table sorting papers.
COOKY

What's all that?

ARTY

Viola's paperwork to get her into school. It will help her
to learn the standard sign language.

COOKY

She won't leave the island.

7.

ARTY

I'll take sign language and correspondence school to her.

I am learning sign too. I will teach you as well.

EXTERIOR: 1958 GREAT BARRIER ISLAND
INTERIOR: BACH BEDROOM—NIGHT
The bach now looks like a lived-in cottage. It has been painted and reconstructed.

VIOLA ARTY COOKY and *MARK* sit around *ARCH'S* bed. *ARCH* is dying.

MARK

We want to take you to hospital.

ARCH

I'm happy to pass into a peaceful nonexistence right here. With my beloved Viola and my best mates.

VIOLA begins to cry. She bends down to *ARCH* and makes guttural noises in his ear.

ARCH

I love you too my darling girl. You are my rock of integrity.

ARCH makes the peace sign with his fingers. *VIOLA* sobs. She climbs onto the bed and cuddles *ARCH*.

COOKY

Vi sweetheart. Time to say goodbye.

EXTERIOR: 1964 QUEEN STREET AUCKLAND—DAY

A massive crowd of protesters walk silently along Queen Street Auckland. People carry banners: 'NO WAR VIETNAM' 'PEACE IN VIETNAM' 'PEACE COMMITTEE PROTEST'. The camera slowly pans into a young woman protester. It is *VIOLA* now 20 years of age. She waves a flag. It reads 'We will never cease to gain peace'. She has a t-shirt which has the New Zealand Sign Language symbol for peace.

8.

INTERIOR: KITCHEN—DAY

COOKY is preparing a meal. *MARK* is at the kitchen table reading the paper. *ARTY* and *VIOLA* sit at the table. They are communicating in sign.

MARK

Listen to this.

MARK beckons *VIOLA*, *COOKY* and *ARTY* to come to the table. *VIOLA* looks over *MARK'S* shoulder and silently reads the paper. *MARK* Reads aloud.

MARK

Viola Baldwin Makes a Big Noise in a Silent Protest. Viola Baldwin, deaf daughter of the late Archibald Baldwin, renowned for his stance as a conscientious objector, was seen waving a large flag with the words 'We will never cease to gain peace'. Viola, a member of the Vietnam Peace Committee had a t-shirt with the New Zealand Sign Language symbol 'Peace'. Although Viola has been deaf all her life, she has been very vocal in her stance as an activist denouncing war and all

186

forms of violence. Viola travels with her companion Artelia Brown who interprets all Viola's New Zealand sign language speeches. The marchers gathered in Aotea Square where Viola 'signed' her protest speech to attract the attention of the New Zealand Government to stop our young men going to Vietnam to die.

COOKY ARTY and *MARK* applaud loudly. *VIOLA* curtsies and signs looking towards the heavens.
VIOLA

I love you, Dad.

FADE OUT:

END

Wind Poem

Paul Barner

todays water
is a polluted green

an obese woman snores in a tent
two children splash and giggle
outside contaminated drain pipes

I say nothing
the woman snores

a beach view
never does much for me

doesn't calm the soul
or bless the eyes

yet
during winter times
at the Gulf

when the wind is cold and sharp
slicing into one side of my face

the ocean, the cliff hanging trees
turn into a vulnerable kindness

it's the cold wind that does that

sprinkles my tension into the sand

*Gulls on the Sand. Image: Melissa
Gunn*

Found in Loss

Susan Glamuzina

Bruce Simpson

Easter 1954

It had been one hundred and twelve days since Dad was killed.

I wouldn't cry anymore. I slid off my coat and tie, sat on the cold yet comfortable leather seats of my green Vauxhall and turned the key.

There had been so much damn press about Dad's death. I wanted to remember my dad—not do an interview! Did the 151 other families feel the same?

I started down the Great South Road alone, leaving the Hauraki Gulf glinting in my rear-view mirror. I was always alone—not out of choice, I just hadn't found anyone worth the compromise that came with being in a relationship. The older I got the less I was willing to change homes or share toilets.

Time to pay tribute to the place Dad took his last breath. I wanted to blame someone for taking Dad on Christmas Eve, ruining future Christmases for all the New Zealanders who'd lost a loved one in the tragic accident, but there was no one at fault. In fact, some heroes tried to stop the train. Heroes who saved many other lives. Why couldn't Dad have been in the last few carriages?

When I arrived at Tangiwai I could smell it—death. The smell lingered even though it had been months. Was it the gases of the lahar that smelled? Whatever it was, it was still death to me.

No one was working on Easter Friday, but the evidence of people building the replacement bridge was everywhere. Piles of rubble and machinery ready for work the next business day. I looked away from the pile of flowers and teddy bears left in remembrance, instead I stared down at the Whangaehu River, still filled with debris. I walked straight ahead, kicked a rock in to the dense terrain and followed it on an untrodden path towards the looming Mt Ruapehu. I kept finding rocks to kick, till one bounced off something turquoise which was half buried.

I hadn't been ready to lose my father. My mother had been taken too early by tuberculosis, a disease I couldn't cure. Dad had died coming to visit me because I was too busy working to travel to him. I wish I'd gone to him. If only I'd sent him money to upgrade to first class, maybe he could've been a survivor. I was the one to blame for his death and would forever be alone —an orphan at twenty-four.

Tangiwai means 'weeping waters', and I could hardly see the river and rocks for tears. I bent down to investigate. A suitcase covered in silt. The leather had started flaking off, but it was still intact. Chances were the suitcase's owner was now deceased; this was my duty. I laid it in my car on the seat beside me. In the morning I would take it to the police.

After work the following day, the turquoise suitcase was still sitting in the evening sun beside my front door on the hallway table. I found myself clicking open the clasps of the case; the smell was volcanic. Aside from a package wrapped up in brown paper and tied with string, there was knitted and cotton clothing, nothing of worth. I slowly pulled the string and lifted out the item from inside the package. It was a silk lavender dress. I knew by the way it'd been wrapped it was special. Taking the dress to the bath, I hand washed it, using Lux flakes like Mum used to, then hanging it outside to dry.

As the clothes dried, I saw Mrs Pearson look over the fence at the women's clothes on my line. Possibly thinking I finally had a lady.

People were always encouraging me to settle down. One day, not yet.

Wiping down the suitcase I discovered a name and wondered, was she still alive? I couldn't reunite with my father but maybe I could reunite this dress with its owner. Before bringing the washing in and settling down to my meal, I wrote a letter to the Evening Post about the suitcase, and specifically the dress. I hoped I could find the owner—Helena Robertson.

Rene Robertson

May 1945

I was in the garden planting my winter vegetables when Valerie from next door walked over.

"Was your mother's name Helena?"

"Yes, why?" I put down my spade.

She held up the Evening Post and started reading.

"*Found, full-length lavender gown in a turquoise suitcase in the bush by the Tangiwai disaster site, believed to have belonged to Helena Robertson.*"

I stood up too fast and my head felt dizzy—or was it Valerie's news? I thought I'd cried the last of my tears, obviously not. I reached out and read the newspaper.

My father was still struggling, drinking too much in my opinion. Dad had told me all about the dress Mum was bringing up on the train on Christmas Eve. She had sat in front of him on the floor hand sewing the dress for hours while they planned their retirement. Mum had not gone with Dad on the train as arranged—because of *that* dress. She hadn't finished sewing the sequins on, and she believed *that* dress would give me my future. She had to stay behind and finish it, so she took a later train—the Christmas Eve train. It was Mum's hope that I would wear it out and find a husband. She was desperate for me to settle down.

I was still looking at the paper, tears smudged the ink of the printed words.

"You can keep it," Valerie said before she headed home.

I put the paper down on the table inside and left it there for a week. Every day it caught my eye until in the end, I wrote to Dad and told him.

Dad's letter back to me was quick, *go get your dress*!

Bruce Simpson

June 1945

The daughter's letter arrived later than I had expected, but when she described the dress, she had it perfect, right down to the wide collar and sequins. The washed dress and other clothes were back in the now clean suitcase, I'd re-wrapped the dress in its brown paper and string.

I drove to her address and parked outside the white villa. I carried the case up the path, past the pink roses and knocked on her door.

"Good afternoon." A beautiful lady, with red hair and forest-green eyes, answered the door.

"Afternoon. I am hoping to meet with Rene Robertson," I said, dipping my black brimmed hat.

"I am Rene," she said. I followed her floral fragrance into the sunny living room, where I handed her the luggage.

Stepping away, I gave her some space to open the case. I stared out the window. It was a magnificent view over to Rangitoto, and out to the Hauraki Gulf. As I gave her time to think about her loss, my loss filled my thoughts too.

I was still watching boats and yachts in the harbour when I felt a hand on my arm. "Thank you so much," she said.

I turned around to see her freckled face glistening with tears.

"My father was on the same train," I told her.

"I'll put the kettle on." She pointed to her dining table, and I made myself comfortable.

Rene Robertson

Valerie helped me put the A-line dress on for my engagement party. My hands ran over the silver-grey and lavender brocade. The diamond ring on my finger sparkled on the cross-over bodice and down the pleated waist.

"Mum did it, Dad," I sobbed. My mother had helped me find a husband from her grave.

Bruce had hand-delivered it to me, but he had given me so much more than just the dress.

The end.

North Wind South of World

Angela Reading

there is always a first
the impact astonishing
my leaping heart
a journey flying high
seeming endless
across the world and then
to arrive in paradise
breathtaking colour
various shades of sea greens
rolling waves topped by
bubbling white foam
translucent yet technicolour
mingled with soft mists
clouds drifting across
vivid blue skies
brilliant islands
resembling
dazzling emerald
and diamond gems
sounds of exotic birds
over the mournful sea

which gently
laps against a ship's bough
protected by taniwha
Ureia the whale
this memory of arrival
a peaceful corridor
of champagne sparkling sea
carrying humanity through
four thousand kilometres
of Tīkapa Moana o Hauraki
a playground for
Auckland's citizens
watched closely
looming high dark and proud
magnificent majestic magical
mysterious chief of all to known in legend as 'sky blood'

Hauraki Gulf Tīkapa Moana. Angela Reading

Out of Her Depth

Josie Laird

Marion is quivering with trepidation as she reaches the wharf, her husband gently coaxing her along. She's managed to remain a landlubber all her life, and she can't believe that it is only now, as an old granny, that she's finally venturing out on the water.

She isn't quite sure where her nervousness has come from. Some long ago TV footage, probably. It hasn't been hard to avoid going out, caught up as she's been with children and home. Her fears haven't stopped Sam from fishing with his mates, and here he is, making her feel like a ninny because she doesn't want to go.

Their kids were pushy about it too. 'You have to go, Mum. You might even like it.'

'I won't,' she'd muttered, but she'd let herself be persuaded.

The boat is huge. A launch, with bedrooms and everything. Even a kitchen. Nothing like what she'd imagined, the tinnies that Sam usually goes out in. Phil shows her around, Marion clutching at doorways while she learns about lifejackets and how to flush the loo.

Then the engines roar into life, Sam unties the ropes, and the boat lurches into action. It takes all the control Marion can muster not to squeal.

'Perfect day for it,' Phil tells her. 'Forecast is settled, water is as smooth as glass. Here Sam, take the wheel while I put the kettle on.'

Marion wants to protest that Sam doesn't know anything about boats like this, but she also doesn't want to show him up in front of his boss. Sam looks happy enough. Maybe it isn't too much different from driving a digger or a truck.

The shoreline looks unrecognisable from out on the water. Phil points out Rangitoto and Waiheke, green-clad oases which separate the dazzling blue of the water from the brilliant blue of the sky. Seabirds flit across the surface of the water which indeed is like a mirror, with only the occasional small wave from other boats to rock theirs.

Marion is starting to relax when there is a loud rattling sound, soon followed by an eerie quiet as the engines die.

'What's wrong?' she asks, looking towards the lifejacket storage.

'Just put the anchor down,' Phil says, grinning. 'I thought we might do some fishing.'

'Yeah,' Sam agrees. 'Now you're talking.' He heads towards the back of the boat. 'Come on Marion, I'll help you get a rod set up.'

Marion eases herself out the back door onto the enclosed deck. 'I think I'll just watch.'

Phil is right behind her. 'You ever caught a fish before?'

'No,' she admits. 'So, I'd probably do it wrong.'

'Not with Sam and me here. We're experts, eh Sam?'

Marion is starting to see why Sam likes working for Phil.

There are all sorts of new words to learn: rod, reel, line, taut, bait, tension. Marion isn't sure she knows what she's doing, but the smelly bit on the end is in the water. Then there's a tug. It gives her a fright, and she thinks about that man who was pulled off his boat into the water by a large fish.

'That's it. One of you blokes can do it now,' she says, trying to pass the rod to Sam. He comes behind her and reaches around to put his hands over hers.

'You can do it, girl,' he whispers in her ear, and shows her how to wind the line in. 'I reckon you've got something on there.'

It's heavy pulling at the end, and then a gorgeous snapper sparkling in pink and silver is flapping about on the deck near her feet. She feels a bit sorry for it. Luckily Phil knows how to put it out of its misery.

'First fish of the day. You've brought us good luck, Marion,' Phil says.

'Can we get a photo for the grandkids?' Sam asks. He lifts the fish into Marion's hands, and she stands there awkwardly while he takes a photo. It's hard to know where to hold it, with its spiky fins and sharp teeth. Now she appreciates how Sam usually brings home fillets, not whole fish.

It isn't only the snapper which has been hooked. Marion is keen to have another go, and the next few hours are spent with lines in the water, and Sam replenishing her bait. She catches a couple more, as does Phil before he descends to the kitchen, or galley as he calls it. He returns with filled rolls and fruit and more cups of tea.

'Right, had enough fishing?' he asks.

'No,' says Marion, giggling with the pleasure of it.

'Perhaps we could try trawling,' he suggests. 'Try for another species, like kingfish or even tuna.'

'Really? What's trawling?'

Sam is already up and taking the bait off the lines. 'We drive the boat slowly along, and put pretend fish on the lines, called lures. Bigger fish come along and snap at them. Hopefully.'

It's just her and Sam out the back now as Phil restarts the engines and pulls up the anchor. Marion grabs hold of the rail when they start moving, but it's a gentle motion and easy enough to stand there.

Then the boat changes direction. Marion can tell, without even looking at the islands. 'What's happening?'

'I'm not sure.' Sam says, and goes inside to ask Phil. He comes out looking like he's found her the best present ever. 'Look over there,' he says, pointing.

'Sharks?' Marion asks as she sees fins break the surface.

'Dolphins,' Sam says.

They pull in their lines and pull out their cameras.

'Over there. Look, there's some more. Oh, a baby one.'

'And there. That's amazing. They're all around the boat.'

Phil comes out and suggests they lie up near the bow and watch the dolphins surf on their wake. Marion isn't sure what he means, but Sam helps her forward and they stay up on the front of the boat, heads over the sides, marvelling as the sleek grey bodies swim alongside the churning water of the boat.

Eventually the dolphins move away, and Marion and Sam heft themselves off the deck and make their way back to the cabin.

'That was amazing,' Marion says. 'Is it like this every time?'

Phil laughs. 'I've never seen that big a pod before,' he says. 'You've brought us good luck, Marion.'

'I can't believe I was scared about coming out,' she says. 'Imagine if I'd missed out on this.'

Sam takes her hand. 'Now you can see why I wanted you to come.'

'Mind you, it's not always like this,' Phil says. 'Right, I think it's time we headed home, if that's okay?'

Marion sighs. 'The kids aren't going to believe what I did today.' She yawns. 'I don't really want it to end.'

She can't believe it herself when she wakes up, the boat gently nudging the wharf. Fancy her going from ultra-nervous to relaxed enough to sleep, all in one day.

What other things has she never tried, too timid to attempt? Maybe she isn't just an old granny after all.

Orakei Wharf. Denise T O'Hagan

Submersion

Edna Heled

Oil on canvas, 2400x1560

Browns Island/Motukorea Sequence

Piers Davies

1
it lies like
a stingray on the
near horizon
a bulging head
the long whiplash tail

2
a knife cut
sears a white line
through the sea
the trees on the tail
sizzle and shimmer

3
enduring summer sun
blurs and smudges
fading into
watercolour hues

4
drought eviscerates
at low-tide
it's a peroxide blonde
rising from the waterline.

5
with passing rain
green shoots
burst through the blonde
and burn out again

6
lost in days of rain
no trace visible
from the waterfront
the volcanic flanks
are moulded in green velvet
substantial in the Winter seas.

Rainy View. Image: Susan Glamuzina

Rakino Island

Lee Simpson

Home Comforts

Sandi Hall

Just before mobile phones connected us, I returned to Auckland from a time of sorrow abroad. Below the plane, I saw at last the eagerly awaited trail of green islands that points to Aotearoa. My mind checked my heart for quivers of known joy. But numbness held me.

Soon after my return, I moved into a marvellous house curved into one of the shallow hillsides above Auckland's inner Hauraki Gulf Harbour. All of its front windows looked out to the water, where little boats seem to dodge between squat, white storage tanks, and Rangitoto backdrops every moment with its blue low-slung cone.

It was there that I fell in love with Millie, an elegantly attractive standard poodle with black, nappy curls covering a well-muscled body. She was as dykely beautiful as her *Special Friend*, Penny.

It was new to me to share my city life with a dog. In my girlhood, I lived on a cattle farm which had several working dogs. Those dogs had such a different air. Because of that, I always feel a stab of pity for large dogs in the city, where they had no function, and no free places to run.

From the first day, I offered to take Millie for runs on the beach and Penny, with a swift assessing glance, replied. "Okay. She'd like that."

Many years before, Penny's family had bought a 50-year lease on the house from the estate of its owner, whose ghost, when I arrived, was still restless in the inner sitting room.

I noticed that Millie often looked at the deep armchair with her ears pricked. But I also knew my sensibilities were stretched almost to breaking point. So I asked Penny about the male presence who seemed to resent my sitting in a certain chair in that room.

"Yep, he's always been there," she affirmed, "but he's harmless. Don't worry about him."

But I did. Death and the transitions to that boundless state had been my university over the past months. I thought of that old man's spirit unable to leave a place that he had perhaps loved, and through my fogged mind came a memory of a Māori wisdom that says the pōhutakawa is the bridge between this world and the mystery beyond.

I said to Penny that I thought a bit of pōhutakawa in the house might release the old man's spirit.

"Good idea," said Pen. Then, after a pause, "Be sure you get permission. Take Millie, if you want."

By now, Millie and I were happy in each other's company and I was finding a great deal of comfort in her constancy. Often, when silent tears were slitting my throat, she'd come to me, look at me briefly, and settle herself against my leg with a throaty grunt.

At Herne Bay, the pōhutakawas had not long finished their blooming. Drifts of their dark red needle-flowers crusted the pale, rumpled sand. Millie was a speck in the distance, a dancing knot against the dazzle of the sea.

I walked beneath the trees, feeling my way. How should I approach the trees? What was the right thing to do?

Millie dashed up to me, eyes brilliant with pleasure, ears like Piglet's in a high wind. She was so eager, I involuntarily laughed. She gave a little dancing jump and rushed off again.

Slowly, I felt drawn to a particular pōhutakawa. I stood in front of it and spoke silently of the old man's spirit. "May I have one of your branches to help him, please?" I said aloud. The small branch near me seemed warm under my hand, and needed almost no pressure to take from the tree.

I put the branch in the corner of the room. Millie sat and looked at it, ears forward, watching something. The next day, I thought the room was warmer than it had been. Over the following weeks, Penny and I agreed that the old man's spirit had gone.

For more than six months, I struggled to be alive in Auckland but at the end of the winter, left it for a fishing village out beyond Matakana, hoping the rhythms of the sea would bring me ease.

Last week, Penny phoned to tell me Millie had died. I felt that lurch of the heart that you do when a beloved has gone. Today, I went to the fishing village beach that had healed me.

Pōhutakawas line the ridge above it, their fiery flowers speaking of life's passion. In the far distance, against the sun dazzle, I thought I saw a black dog dancing.

Dazzled. Image: Melissa Gunn

Young Fish, Old Fish

Justine Newnham

'Jeffery! Someone's at the door!' Geraldine screamed.

'OK, OK!' Jeffery wasn't expecting any more guests today. He already had a 'surprise' visitor in the lounge, his father. Jeffery hadn't seen his father since his mother died, over ten years ago. Their relationship had become strained after her death and they hadn't talked to each other since.

This surprise visit had Jeffery worried that something might be wrong with his dad. Although he looked fit, he was getting on. Jeffery had forgotten how old he was. All he remembered was that he was much younger than his mother, who had unexpectedly died in her mid-sixties. Jeffery's son, Joel, was just about to start school at the time. His mother had really adored Joel.

Jeffery was too worried about himself getting old to think about his father's problems. Hitting forty was a bit of a shock. His body was changing beyond his control. He was more concerned about his expanding beer belly than his increased blood pressure. He ignored the doctor harping on about his high blood pressure, although he knew he should be concerned as that was what killed his mother. He just tried to block out those body changes by hanging on to his youthfulness.

Unfortunately, this way of thinking led him down a path of sleeping with gorgeous young twenty-somethings, not much older than his son. It felt good at the time but he regretted it now. Especially since his wife, Geraldine, found out. His second marriage down the drain. Geraldine was currently packing up all her things and would be moving in with her sister this weekend. He didn't know how he would live without her. She was his rock. Deep down, Jeffery felt a need to make changes in his life, but that was not the kind of change he wanted. The whole situation felt like he had lost control of his life somehow. Especially when the young girl texted him to meet up again. And knew he should really block her number. He tried to forget about her as he walked up to the front door to open it. He was surprised to see his fifteen-year-old son, Joel, and his ex-wife, Sarah standing there.

'Hi, could Joel hang out with you for the weekend?' Sarah asked.

'OK. Are you going away with *him* again?' Jeffery didn't like Sarah's new boyfriend.

'Yes, why not?' Sarah shrugged.

'Come in Joel' Jeffery grabbed Joel's bag. 'Your Grandad and I are just about to go fishing in the Hauraki Gulf. Do you remember Grandad?'

'Yes,' replied Joel.

'You're talking to your father now? That's great,' Sarah looked at Jeffrey.

'I thought it would be a great opportunity to try out my new boat. Better to fish in company. Just hope his surprise visit is not to tell me has cancer or something.'

'I saw your boat. Where does Geraldine park her car?' Sarah probed.

'Well, she and I are not doing so well,' Jefferey said, quietly.

'Oh dear.' Sarah turned and walked down the driveway.

Joel followed Jeffery down the hallway and into the lounge where Jack sat.

'Hey Dad, guess who is here? Joel. This should be good a fishing trio,' Jeffery announced.

Joel gave his grandad a big hug, which surprised Jeffery. He didn't think Joel would remember him. Joel was only five at the time they stopped talking to each other. It seems like he missed him. Guilt sweeps over Jeffery. It had been a difficult time for him as he was going through a horrible divorce with Joel's mother and at the same time his father was seeing a young lady which had made him angry as his mother had only just passed away. Jeffery couldn't handle the whole situation.

It was a fine day for fishing. The water was dead still and not a cloud in the sky. Many people must have thought the same thing. So many boats on trailers lined up ready to back down the ramp at Takapuna Beach. A few boats looked the same as his. Maybe they bought their boat last weekend at the Boat Show too. He hoped there are some newbies to the boating world like he was. He didn't want to look like the only person not knowing what he was doing.

It was Jeffery's turn to back his boat trailer down the ramp. He felt nervous as he'd never backed a trailer before. Many people are waiting so he felt extra pressure to hurry. The trailer didn't go where it was supposed to go, but he eventually managed to make it to the bottom of the ramp. Not straight though. But it didn't matter as now it was in the water. Next, he had to park the trailer somewhere. He left his son and father on the boat while doing that.

Main task achieved. Boat in the water. One of Jeffery's biggest worries was his inability to tie knots. Because of that he planned not to dock anywhere. All he could imagine was his knots coming loose and the boat drifting off, out into the Hauraki Gulf somewhere. Never to be seen again.

'Better get on with our fishing adventure,' Jeffery tried to shake that image from his mind.

There was silence as the boat drove away from the beach. The whole *City of Sails* shrank on the horizon as they sailed further and further out into the vast world of blue. Islands that usually looked small from the mainland expanded into new shapes as they moved into a new perspective. There was something magical about being amongst the usually distant islands. Each one was unique. Joel started taking lots of photos with his phone.

'Have you been on a boat before, Joel?' Jeffery asked.

'Not a small one like this,' Joel replied.

"It's such a great feeling leaving the land behind and being up close to the ocean, the fresh air, the sea birds, and the fish of course. We are so blessed with this amazing Hauraki Gulf just on our doorstep,' Jeffery mused.

They sailed up close to the largest island from the mainland, Rangitoto.

'Do you know much about this island, son?' Jeffery asked.

'Not really,' Joel replied.

'It is supposed to be Auckland's youngest volcano,' Jeffery lectured. 'It only erupted about 600 years ago. May seem like a long time ago, but it is not in terms of volcano years.'

'What! Did it erupt like Whakaari did a few years back?'

'Sort of. But it was much more violent. Don't worry, it's supposed to be dormant,' Jeffery corrected.

'Oh, that's good.' Joel looked relieved.

'Anyway, let's fish,' Jeffery puts down the anchor and grabbed three fishing rods. One each. Then Jeffery grabbed a large 'Crocodile Dundee' like knife. He opened the chilly bin, stuck his hand in the ice and pulled out a large bag full of fish bait. Cut open the bag with one swipe of the large knife and pulled out a small fish from the bag. He chopped it into three parts.

'There you go. One each.' He stuck the hook through the small fish's head. 'This, my son, is the finest bait one can buy. Only kidding. Just got it from the service station on the way here.' Jeffery turned to see Jack roll his eyes.

'Why buy this expensive boat if you don't really know how to fish?' Jack scoffed. 'Are you trying to get attention from those young girls? Geraldine told me about your fling.'

'Dad. Not in front of Joel,' Jeffery muttered. 'I am not sure what is happening to me. Since I hit forty I can feel my body and my mind is changing. I want to make changes in my life. Not sure I could do that with Geraldine. She is much older than me. Too stuck in her ways and a bit controlling, too. Anyway, you did the same thing when Mum died. You hooked up with that young lady nearly the same age as me. And why did you want to catch up with me today? Are you dying?' Jeffery tried to divert the negative attention away from himself.

'No! But, that lady you are talking about, Julie. She and I want to get married,' Jack replied.

'You're what?' Jeffery's eyes rolled.

'Dad!' Joel butted in. 'Don't be mean. You're mean to Grandad. Mean to Geraldine and apparently you were mean to mum many years ago.'

'Look Jeffery,' Jack spoke up. 'Your mother was my rock and I miss her every day. When she passed, I felt like my entire world disappeared. I hit rock bottom. Didn't want to tell you how bad I felt. Just didn't talk about things like that back then. Julie saved me. I don't know how I would have coped without her.'

An uncomfortable silence took over as all three watch their cast lines move with the motion of the water.

'I was hoping to see a dolphin,' Jeffery broke the silence.

'What happened to becoming a marine biologist?' Jack asked Jeffery. 'You were fascinated with dolphins as a child.'

'Too old for studies now,' Jeffery replied.

'You're not too old,' said Jack.

'Maybe,' Jeffery changed the topic again. 'When are you having that wedding? Are we invited?'

'Definitely, I want you both to join us on our special day,' Jack replied.

'Hey guys, hate to interrupt, but what's happening to my line?' Joel suddenly yelled.

Jeffery and Jack turned to see Joel's fishing rod bent in half.

'What do I do? I can't hold it for much longer!' Joel screamed. Jeffery runs to help Joel hold the fishing rod.

'Holey Moley, that's a feisty one,' Jeffery shouted. 'Not sure I can hold it, too. Dad, we need your help!'

Jack ran over to assist. Suddenly all three men were hugging each other while holding onto Joel's fishing rod.

'Gosh, we haven't been this close together in years,' Jeffery joked.

'Be serious, Dad! What do I do?' Joel yelled. 'We can't stay like this forever!'

Jeffery didn't know what to do. The fish at the end of the line was putting up a decent fight, it wanted to survive so badly. It played a game of tug of war with the three men, tricking them into thinking it was relaxing and then suddenly pulling on the line again. The sudden jolts nearly sent all three men into the water many times. It was like being on a bucking bull in a rodeo. None of them wanted the fish to win. Not a good story to tell people on the land, that the fish got away. Unfortunately, the men were not winning this game. It was only a matter of time before someone ended up in the water.

'It sure is a beast. Kahawai put up a great fight. I remember as a boy watching my brother struggling to reel in a kahawai off a wharf at Island Bay,' Jack said.

'It's like a Taniwha. The guardian of the Hauraki Gulf,' Jeffery added.

'Dad, I can't handle this anymore!' Joel yelled again.

Jeffery had enough too. He reached for the large knife, swung it to the top of the fishing rod and cut the line in two, sending all three men flying backwards, landing on top of each other. Jack and Joel looked at each other and burst into laughter.

'Had to let the Taniwha go,' Jeffery said, shrugging his shoulders. The others continue to laugh. 'Not sure if this fishing thing is for me. Why did I buy this boat again?'

'To catch young fish,' Jack joked.

Jeffery shrugged again.

'I think I need to stop trying to be someone else. Accept my age, accept myself.'

'A change in thought. Maybe that's the change you are looking for.' Jack patted Jeffery on his shoulder.

'I didn't realise you were so wise, Dad.' Jeffery smiled back at his father.

Have You Ever Collected Stories from a Windbag?

John Leyland

My Uncle Peter, in his 101st year, delighted in telling, retelling and re-retelling us his stories. I captured a few as they zipped by and put them on a website and in a book. He said, 'I love roaming around in my mind'. One day, after he roamed, he told me, 'sometimes our family scratched a bit, but we never starved. But my grandfather, Old Phil, he nearly did, on Great Barrier Island, when his father took the family over there. 1860s. His mother's kitchen was a canvas thrown over the branch of a tree. Storms. The boats couldn't get in. The local Maoris showed them how to survive by eating pipis and thistles. Milk-thistle, that is. Pūhā.' I needed to check that out, so, off to search the digitised newspapers at the National Library website. I searched for 'Old Phil's' father: Edward Leyland, who took his family, including 'Old Phil', then aged about 12, to the Great Barrier in 1867. A deluge of information!!

1859. Edward arrived in NZ from Yorkshire.

1862. Edward's wife, Emma, arrives with their two children. One of their kids was Uncle Peter's grandfather, 6 year old Phil.

1863. In January, Edward took part in the second race of the Anniversary Regatta. The competitors were 18 sailing vessels under 5 tons. Edward was self-employed as a 'General Shipping Agent' and 'Customs Broker' agent in Auckland.

1864. Edward was appointed Auckland's first Inspector of Weights and Measures and Inspector of Bread. The Bread Act had been passed in 1863, aimed at ensuring bread was up to quality and weight specifications.

1866. Hard times arrived. Auckland was in a depression. To feed his family Edward embezzled one pound, for which crime he spent 3 months in Mt Eden prison. He was released in December. It was time for a change of location and profession.

1867. Edward was declared bankrupt. Edward's brother in law, James Reade had a farm on The Barrier. Maybe this family connection inspired Edward to plan the establishment of a 'Tryphena Hotel' at the port. Edward drafted a petition and obtained six signatures from the masters of coastal trading vessels that called at Great Barrier Island to escape treacherous weather. His application for a 'bush licence' was successful. Full of hope, the family headed off to the island but the weather was against them. His plan fails and soon he is forced to recross the gulf to Thames to operate the Courthouse Hotel. I know that 'Old Phil's' brother, John, as a teenager, travelled back across the gulf from Thames to The Barrier in 1870 to 'look after' the Reade's farm. Why the farm needed 'looking after' and exactly where it was, I'd love to know. But there my story, sadly, stops. The curtain has come down....

Nothing Ventured

Estelle Geddes

'Take the whole school to explore the Hauraki Gulf? Are you sure this will work?'

'Of course.'

She'd organised this outing three times already, at her previous school, with great success. This, however, was a very different community.

The day arrived, warm and sunny. Walking through the school gates, she stared in disbelief. Instructions had been clear. There was room for only ten extra adults but every family member, young and old, who was free that day, had turned up in anticipation.

'It's going to be cool, eh Miss,' a teenager grinned, jostling her with his arm. 'Hey, look. Bus driver's calling to you.'

Panic-stricken, she walked over.

'This happens all the time,' the driver grinned. 'We'll cram them in, no problem,' and soon the buses were on their way.

Children gasped and clapped when they saw the ferry waiting, just for them.

She had her apologies ready but the staff were very relaxed.

'Lots of the kids' rellies work for Fullers so we knew this would happen. Fullers won't go broke and the ferry won't sink, so no worries.'

Everyone cheered and boats hooted as they headed out to the Gulf. Nearing the container cranes, the ferry slowed. The mother of one of the children worked there. In unison, the crane arms rose then lowered in salute. Everyone clapped and yelled in response.

They cruised towards Motukorea Island, then circled out and round, heading past Devonport. The commentary gave loads of information. The children swivelled this way and that, absorbed by every detail. Silence fell as the ferry headed towards the Harbour Bridge. It stopped underneath.

'Oh wow!' One student spoke for them all.

They poured off the boat at Devonport, erupting from the terminal on to the footpath. The buses were waiting. That wasn't part of the plan. She turned to the Principal.

'If we march through Devonport,' he whispered, 'they'll call out the armed guard.'

So, once again, everyone crammed on board to drive the two-minute journey to the foot of Mount Victoria. Elderly grandparents trudged up the steep slopes without a word of complaint, flapping their straw hats to keep them cool. It was certainly worth the effort.

They identified the islands and the places they'd passed but some children were very concerned. The islands had shrunk.

'And so has our boat,' someone else observed.

'But we haven't, have we?'

Another excellent teaching moment.

Eventually and reluctantly, they headed back to the buses, returning to school over the Harbour Bridge, a new experience for many and a chance to explore another view of the Gulf.

'Well, it certainly was a great success,' the Principal smiled broadly, 'but I have to admit I thought you were stark raving mad.'

'And I've been thinking about our next trip. We could explore Rangitoto and Motutapu islands?'

She didn't catch his response.

Ferry Trip. Image: Melissa Gunn

The Story of Spot X: My Waitematā Story

Mitchell Thorburn

This story tells of how my Dad and I, whom I scuba dive and free dive with, both in our free time and for the conservation projects we're involved with, discovered a spot that would inspire hope to both the locals of Waiheke Island and the greater Hauraki Gulf/Tīkapa Moana.

It all begins two weeks after day 107 of the Delta lockdown—freedom at last. We took the opportunity to do just a fun dive off the northern coast of Waiheke Island. Super excited, as always, we packed our vessel 'Mylio' (a 5.5m Centre Console RIB) and headed to the dive site for the day.

This dive site in particular was one of the few full leather kelp/rimurimu (*Ecklonia radiata*) forests left off the northern coast of Waiheke. Kina/sea urchin barrens weren't as common as other parts of the Gulf. We started our dive, and like every dive I do, I was filming and photographing the best of what the site had to offer. Schools of sweep, parore and red moki filled the underwater space.

But something else caught our eye. We moved over to what looked like collapsed arch in the reef and see upon close inspection that it's not just an arch, but an active packhorse lobster/kōura nest. What made this special was the number found at once. We noted more than 10 kōura which is rare for Waiheke. I filmed and photographed the nest while my Dad noted down observations of the habitat discovered.

After the dive ended, we named this dive site 'Spot X' and have kept the real location a secret to this day. Only us and a few trusted others know the true location of the best kōura/lobster habitat we've seen in a long time.

The take-away message is if we allow marine protections to occur, find ways to sustainably harvest seafood/kaimoana and allow marine reefs to regenerate; it will benefit both us and the surrounding environment for future generations to come.

Wave. Acrylic on canvas. Susan Glamuzina

Night Vision

Susan Glamuzina

I look west to the city
glowing with action
from Tāmaki Drive
where bricks were hand laid
by men who have since moved on
hidden from my vision
but my imagination draws them in place
I look east in the dark
and see a handful of fairy lights
my eyes can't see the islands
Rangitoto, Waiheke, Browns, Rakino
Great Barrier, and the Coromandel
hidden from my vision
but my imagination draws them in place
I look out in the harbour
all I see is black waves
I can't see the wildlife
whales, dolphins, blue penguins, seals
fish, turtles and plankton
hidden from my vision
my imagination draws them in place
Surrounded by seas, land and volcanoes

Auckland has so much to offer
I know the peaks and the valleys
with no moon or sunlight
hidden from my vision
still my imagination draws them in place
I look towards the beach
imagining the future
building sandcastles and pushing swings
with children yet to be born
hidden from my vision
still my imagination draws them in place

Night Vision. Image: Susan Glamuzina

Turn of the Tide

Juliet Yates

The locals always called the little village *the Bay*. Mum would say 'I'm off to the Bay, to get a library book, shoe repairs, needles and cottons, crochet hooks, candles for the power cuts, coils of flypaper, tiny mouse traps'. Local shops, where you could buy almost anything—things which Mark suspects no one needs now.

After shopping, Mum would send the children to run to the beach and play in their paradise, swimming or fishing. Day-long picnics with endless time to make sandcastles, ponds, canals, and draw strange designs which lasted until the tide turned and waves came in.

Back from Aussie, Mark had returned to the Bay. Wanting to see the places of his childhood and the family that he once had, and the beach where he used to play. Places of adventures and happenings. He could not find them all. He saw that small village houses had been renovated or demolished and their replacements marched up the nearby hills.

No wonder, he thought, as he walked past estate agents' offices. They advertised St Heliers as 'one of the most beautiful suburbs of Auckland with one of the most popular beaches, just fifteen minutes from the heart of the city, but retaining its original seaside charm and identity'. The Bay that Mark once knew so well.

As a child, Mark would wake early, follow his father down to the beach and watch the sun rise above the shoulder of Rangitoto Island.

He would dig in the sand, uncover insects and sea lice, scavenging among the seaweeds thrown up by high tide, and sniff the kelp, mingled with the tang of discarded fish heads and guts where seagulls squabbled. He startled crabs hidden under Dad's upturned dinghy. It was a one-man boat, clinker-built with over-lapping wooden planks, strong but not too heavy so Dad could lift it. Dad would test the wind direction with his wetted finger and sniff the air. If it was good for fishing, he'd have ready his net and lines, box of hooks and sinkers, anchor and oars. Then he would untie the painter from the seawall, and stoop low, putting his shoulders under the dinghy.

"Hey Dad! Where are you going?" Mark calls, running towards him.

"Motutapu."

"Can I come?"

"Not this time. Out of the way, you little tyke. This boat is heavy."

"But you promised I could come."

"Not today. If it blows up you will end up grizzling about being cold, wet, sick, and nag about getting home. You can fish from the beach. You've got your own line."

Dad slowly lifts the boat and walks down the beach. His legs stick out like the claws of a hermit crab, dragging its house along. His feet dig deep holes in the sand. He drops the boat in the water, eases his shoulders and fixes the oars in rowlocks. Crabs, evicted from their refuges in the seaweed scuttle down to the sea.

Mark kicks the sand, turns over empty shells. No way can he catch snapper off the beach. He follows Dad into the water and watches him row into the sun. Little waves flick in and out as the tide creeps down the sand. Mark's toes turn wrinkled and white. The boat is just a speck, away past Rangitoto to Islington Bay, or Drunken Bay as Dad and his yachtie mates used to call it. It was Dad's favourite fishing spot near Motutapu. Now it's the finish line for classic yacht races.

"Hey Mark! Get some pipis!" Tom and Brian call from the village. They are followed by the girl from the house on the cliff. Her name is Ginny. She smiles, screwing up her freckled face and tossing her red curls. Tagging along behind her is *Little Sister*. Mark sees her for the first time.

"Why did you bring her? She's too little."

"Mum made me," said Ginny.

Little Sister is left to play in the sand. The boys and Ginny wade out to the shellfish beds where they scrabble under the sand to fill their buckets. Searching for pipis and cockles. Sometimes they light a fire from driftwood and eat shellfish on the beach, but today Mum had said to hurry back with Little Sister. It is low tide so the boys crawl inside the huge stormwater drainpipe, which is a shortcut under the road. They leave Ginny and Little Sister, covered in sand, to scramble home up the cliff track.

Wriggling out of the drain, the boys wander along the creek lined with flax and rushes. They hear wings flutter and bird calls. Tūī dance on the flax flowers, sipping nectar. The sun gleams on the green leaves pointed like spears. The boys dodge in and out of the flax and hide from Mr Jackson, the returned soldier who lives across the creek. He has propped up an old launch on its cradle under a corrugated iron lean-to. Mark goes as close as he dares. The old boat is a long way from the sea. He wonders will it ever taste saltwater again, feel the tug of waves, or list and tilt in the changing wind? Or must it, like the owner, see out its days stranded so far from the tide?

Mark sees Mr Jackson struggling with a tin of paint, stumbling a little on his crutches. He is on an endless mission, scraping and sanding down the old boat, repainting its clinkered planks.

The boys call a shy hello.

"How old is he?" whispers Brian.

"Must be 100."

"Where is his leg?"

"They cut it off in the war."

"What's war?"

"Fighting, like this." They laugh as Mark pushes Brian over.

Lois Jackson brings a cup of tea for her dad. She watches the scuffle get serious. She calls "That's enough. You boys! Get home." They race off up the track.

Mark remembers how he met the boys. It was first day of school. A day of strangeness, teacher commands scarcely understood, new entrants cringing when older pupils laughed at their mistakes. Mark thinks of that year as a timeless zone. Tomorrows were yesterdays and each day the same.

When he was not in school, he met the boys at the beach, gathering shellfish, making sand towers, trickling sand through their fingers.

They wanted to explore further, but upstream the creek was untamed. Floods carved new courses through the Dingle Dell Reserve, so kids had to be cautious. No one went far up stream. They had been warned about the Taniwha who lives there waiting to grab a strange traveller or lost kid.

Today, 20 years later, Mark finds no sign of the creek. He guesses that it has been sent underground in a vast stormwater system. Townhouses cram the land where baches once sheltered under apple trees beside the creek. Asphalt covers the muddy tracks he used to tread.

There is still beach, but no dumps of empty shells. New fine sand. Dredged from offshore. The beach is fringed by Auckland Council notices about dog-walking times, the safe swimming lane, and rules for use of the boat ramp where Mark sees several parked vehicles. The ramp bisects the curve of the Bay and gives access for jet skis, kayaks, and small runabouts with fast outboard engines. Mark finds no wooden dinghies ribbed like cockle shells. No-one is painstakingly rowing out to fish in the Rangitoto channel. He guesses that no-one would dare to leave their craft near the ramp overnight these days.

As the wind rises, Mark gazes at windsurfers, kite-surfers, hang-gliders appearing from all over Auckland. Kite-surfers race across the Bay turning against the wind and capsizing in the gusts. Hang-gliders arrive, swoop low as the wind changes and land carefully on the beach. Mark reaches the seawall. Someone, not the locals, but strangers with knives have searched for barnacles and scraped it clean. There are no rock oyster shells and no baby mussels. How can anyone be satisfied killing a generation of shell-fish, Mark asks himself. Newcomers don't understand, Council prohibition notices are too late.

Mark takes off his shoes and tests the water. Drifting fingers of green, slimy eel grass clutch his ankles. Silt and mud squelch between his toes turning them into white and grey bones—like the sprats he once caught for the cat.

The only thing Mark finds the same is Rangitoto. No politician had persuaded the council to allow developers on the green volcano, but new buildings were permitted to plaster the cliffs surrounding the Bay and along Tamaki Drive with apartment blocks. He looks across the road. The historic Grand Hotel is now a glass fronted drinking palace. Tables and chairs clutter the footpath. He checks the outdoor menu. Outrageous prices for snapper and chips, and warnings that fish depend on the catch. Instead of local cockles or pipis, the next cafes promise South Island oysters or imported prawns.

Mark hurries to meet Ginny, the only one of the gang who stayed in the Bay and kept in touch. He walks past the stormwater pipe. The mouth is covered with a safety grid. No one can climb inside it now. He looks at the outfall, which used to be a huge pipe open at the low tide mark. A pile of rocks has been dumped over the pipe and concreted together to look like a natural outcrop. Children climb up the sides, looking for pools with anemones left by the outgoing tide.

At last, here is Ginny. Mark hesitates, then gives her a big hug.

"So glad to see you. You look great," he says. "You 're just the same, but the Bay is not the place we once knew."

"Yes, I know. So many changes. New visitors, new residents, new needs and demands on the beach."

The sun is high. Rangitoto no longer shadows the water. Under the pōhutukawa, Mark and Ginny watch an extended family unpack picnic baskets, toys, towels, and surfboards. Children with long, braided hair rush to the playground and climb into the old, blue dinghy fastened securely there. It is their favourite. They jostle for the oars and pretend to row over the concrete to the island. Going fishing, like their father.

Mark and Ginny watch the family's SUV backing slowly down the ramp, launching a runabout with two high-powered outboards, life jackets and outriggers for the fishing rods. The sun has dried out the eel grass, so it no longer beckons and waves. The runabout powers towards the channel between Rangitoto and Motutapu, and Drunken Bay. Mark wonders, will these newcomers keep clear of the taniwha? Do they know the stories? A protector taniwha for each motu? The wind mixes the smell of salt and seaweed with whiffs of fuel from the outboards. Will that disguise the scent of strangers and perhaps keep the Taniwha at bay?

Aunties call the children and head to the shops for ice creams. Not walking on the beach, but on the Council board walk. It runs round the waterfront. Ginny laughs when a tour bus arrives.

"Tourists can see the beaches and do not take off their shoes. They never feel the sand between their toes or run with the wind in their hair. "

Mark grasps Ginny's hand.

"I was devastated to learn about Little Sister. Her voice was amazing, and her style unique. She decorated her dress with offerings from the sea: pipi shells, feathers, beads and strands of seaweeds, crab shells."

"She loved the songs you sent her. But you stopped writing," said Ginny.

"She did not want me to. She found a new man to enhance her talent."

"He gave her something all right. They found her on the beach, covered with sand. Collapsed, with an overdose."

"Tragedy. Unbearable."

"Mark, you should publish the songs."

"My music is stashed with her sketches somewhere in your garage. I can't bear the thought of going back there. Too many reminders."

"Time to move on, Mark."

"Time does not move. Just scuttles like a hermit crab up the beach looking for an empty shell. If it's lucky, once or twice a year a spring tide reaches it and washes it into deep water."

Mark's eyes burn with tears. He agonises over the intense time he had spent with Little Sister. She called herself Sand when performing. She sang of treacherous currents, rippling as the tide turns. And fickle winds, creating waves to caress or pound the shore. He wondered had she'd been happy as a child, on the beach? Singing to the sound of the sea, sketching in the sand. Waiting for the kids to come and take her home.

Mark and Ginny watch a distant runabout. It veers too close to cliffs, disappears between the islands. The tide has turned. White capped waves and rising wind promise a rough passage.

Mark's dad did not return from fishing in Drunken Bay. His clinker-built cockle shell was lost. Mark and Ginny remember the Taniwha. Protector of the motu.

Okioki i runga i te rangimarie   Rest in peace

Settlements

Lincoln Jaques

We stepped ashore that day
although we were not the first—
Ngai Tai & Te Kawerau fought
fierce battles with Ngāti Whātua
down on the beaches of Onewa
and Ngāti Paoa who rowed across
from Waiheke, traversed the Hauraki
for skirmishes on the northern shores
of the Waitematā. Those many bodies
washed in the mosquito swamps of Onepoto.

Rain fell and brought the clay sludge
ruiningly down from the hills
where they'd raped the 1,000-year-old
Kauri, their bodies boxed into coffin houses
where we all moved our few belongings
into, waited for our untimely deaths.

We bunched with another family
into a Californian bungalow, its ribs breaking
view of Rangitoto and the horizon
where those first waka broke through

later the white sails of bubonic ships.
They too stepped ashore, walked up these slopes
the flies crawling into their wishbones.
My earliest memory is laying on the bunk
cloth-sack style mattress, like a Fencible
call of the ruru through the tōtara. The tears.

On the morning of our first day I awoke
early. A different sun bled through the worn
curtain. In the corner of the sash window
a spider had cast its web. The first light
drew a map of the rest of my life.
Sunstrokes of lost worlds made silent.

Contributor Biographies

AGE Virtual School In 2024 AGE Virtual students took a deep dive into creative writing. The Hauraki Gulf is such a special environment to contemplate, ideate and explore with the students readily writing, drafting, editing and excitedly sharing their new found skill set.

Alexandra Balm. Alexandra writes poems, short stories, and literary studies. She received several awards and fellowships. Her work was published in Aotearoa New Zealand and overseas. She taught at the Universities of Cluj and Otago. Garry Forrester called her "mother of metamodernism" in his 2014 memoir. She lives in South Auckland, where she teaches high school English.

Alexandra Fraser has lived in the beautiful Tāmaki Makaurau most of her life. She has been published in NZ and overseas for years and is working on her third collection. Previous collections are Conversation by Owl light, and StarTrails (both published by Steele Roberts Aotearoa).

Amanda Eason. Poet/teacher Amanda Eason has 4 collections published by NZ and UK poetry presses. Her work has appeared in numerous magazines and anthologies in both countries e.g. NZ - Landfall, The Listener. UK - The Observer, New Statesman and Society. Amanda co-convenes *Titirangi Poets* monthly at Titirangi Library and gives readings and workshops.

Andrew Holdaway is a remote sensing scientist living in Auckland. With a love of Auckland's coastline and beaches, he enjoys exploring them from both the ground and by using satellite imagery, which can provide unique perspectives on the natural beauty of the New Zealand landscape.

Angela Campbell is a scribbler based in Auckland, New Zealand. For any success that she has, she wishes to acknowledge Mrs Bull, her primary school teacher (whose encouragement fanned the flames of Angela's passion for writing) and all dedicated educators whose passion for teaching makes a difference in the lives of children.

Angela Reading has lived in Auckland New Zealand since 1974, and is originally from London England. She came to creative writing late in life as a mature student, when studying Fine Arts at Elam, Auckland University. She is a painter, poet, and performance artist.

Angela Vuletich is an abstract artist based in Auckland. Instagram: @angevuletich

Anni Docking is a New Zealand poet, wordsmith and social entrepreneur. Graduating from University of Auckland in 2016, her B.A. (Hons) in English Literature and Education complements her Diploma of Business Studies from Massey University. She finds artistic inspiration from the ocean and is currently weaving a nautical poetry collection. Anni is a member of the New Zealand Society of Authors: https://authors.org.nz/author/annette-docking/

Atlas Wrathall. Atlas loves to sing, dance and compose lyrics. He is fascinated by words and how they work together. Being outdoors brings him joy. The Hauraki Gulf is his happy place; searching for treasure, splashing in the waves, designing sand castles and swinging in trees, fills his bucket to the moon back and beyond.

Bog Bakaric was born and raised in West Auckland. He wrote his first short story during lockdown and has now written for all three Auckland Writers anthologies.

Brian John Evans lives in Auckland, born in 1933. All his poems can be seen at his site: http://www.bestpoet.com

Britney Mathias holds a postgraduate diploma in marine science from the University of Auckland, and is passionate about conservation education, particularly human interactions with seals and sea lions.

Bron van der Geest. Bron is a passionate advocate for the Hauraki Gulf. She has swam, explored and gazed out upon its waters and treasure trove of islands, for over 5 decades. Recently she has been sailing across it's expanse and is loving every magical memory making movement.

Bruce Wyness grew up in a small country town close to beaches, rivers, ranges and farmland. Experiences from this time are reflected in his writing, mainly short fiction but also reimagined and retelling family history. He is an avid reader observer of people and uses that to craft his stories.

Caroline Carlyle. A poet, writer, and artist, Caroline was raised in a literary-loving family. An active member of various writing groups such as I.W.W. NZ, she has claimed awards such as an Emerging Poet Award in the Kathleen Grattan Competition 2016, and a 2023 runner-up in the Michele Whitecliffe Art Writing Prize.

Chantelle Van Vuuren (she/her) grew up in Tāmaki Makaurau and daydreams about being a full-time writer in her law lectures. She likes to write poems and record eighteen-minute-long voice memos instead of sharing her feelings with her friends.

Christopher Reed is a high school English teachers from Auckland. He is an award winning writer, musician and teacher with a beautiful wife and two wonderful daughters. Being a part of the Auckland Writer's collections has been a real honour.

Darian Smith lives in Auckland, New Zealand with his wife (who also writes) and their Siamese cat (who doesn't). He has a degree in psychology and English, a Diploma of Counselling, and is a member of the New Zealand Association of Counsellors. He has won prizes for short stories and a novel and been a finalist for the Sir Julius Vogel Award three times. For more information about Darian and his upcoming work, please check out his website at www.darian-smith.com

Denise T O'Hagan attained an MCW in 2016 from AUT. She enjoys writing poetry and fiction and is working on several novels. Her poems have been published in Fresh Ink Anthology, NZ Poetry Society Anthology, Fast Fibres Poetry, The Blue Nib, Tarot and Takahē magazine.

Edna Heled is an artist, art therapist, counsellor and travel journalist living in Auckland. She studied Film & TV (BFA), Visual Arts (Diploma), Art Therapy (MA) and Psychology (BA Hons). Her writing includes short stories, poetry, travel writing and non-fiction. She is widely published in NZ, Australia, USA, UK, and more.

Élise Cater is a keen tween writer of fantasy who loves cats and herbs. She also enjoys pencil and watercolour art. She grew up on the shores of the Hauraki Gulf. She likes writing about forests, so this story about the sea is a bit out of her comfort zone.

Elizabeth Morton is a yarn teller and neuroscience enthusiast from Tāmaki Makaurau. Her latest collection of poetry is Naming the Beasts (Otago University Press, 2022).

Estelle Geddes loves writing. Her first poem was published aged 6, four lines of angst inspired by her toddler brother! She enjoys writing in a variety of genres and styles, and for all age groups. Estelle has published poems, fiction, travel stories, biographies and a book review.

Gretchen Carroll lives in Tāmaki Makaurau, Aotearoa, with her husband and son. She has worked in journalism and communications for more than 20 years, and enjoys writing flash fiction. More on her online writing portfolio: https://gretchencarroll.journoportfolio.com/

Jackson Lowe. Jackson is a 19 year old who enjoys writing poetry in his own time and style. Writing became a hobby of his at 16 as all he needed was a pen and paper. He does not consider himself to be a poet but he tries.

Jenny Clay is a poet, sometime artist, fiction and non-fiction writer. She has been published in Fresh Ink, Poetry Pudding, Flightpath, This Twilight Menagarie, in Titirangi Poets and New Zealand Poetry Society anthologies, Takahe, Poetry NZ, and More than a Roof; and on various ezines.

Jeremy Redmore is an award-winning songwriter, children's book author and educator who has spent more than half his life living on, exploring and being inspired by the vast shores of the Hauraki Gulf. This is his first published piece of poetry.

John Leyland. John was born in Palmerston North but has lived in Hamilton, Taupo and Auckland while enjoying varied careers, such as managing a department store, training Kindergarten teachers, running a bonsai nursery, making pottery and being a ferry-boat waiter. Since 1978 he's been besotted with family history. John loves both historical fiction and truth. https://paperspast.natlib.govt.nz/ http://roamingaroundinmymind.weebly.com263

Josie Laird has experienced some fantastic days out on the harbour, and some miserable ones too. She's a novelist and short story writer, a boatie and a gardener.

Juliet Yates, MNZM, former solicitor and city councillor, grew up in St Heliers sailing classic yachts with her father, and explored the islands of the Gulf. She supports the Hauraki Gulf Marine Park Protection Bill and hopes it will ensure future generations enjoy this wonderful place.

Justine Newnham works as a full-time gardener and studies horticulture part time. In her spare time, she likes to write. She wrote a short story and a couple poems for the last Anthology of

Dominion Road. She was diagnosed with dyslexia late in life and wants to encourage other neurodiverse people to give writing a go too.

Karen Morris-Denby. 'Every second that passes by, you will never get back. This has always fascinated me', Niuean writer Karen says. 'I like to capture a moment and create a visual image with words. This helps my imagination run in every direction'. Karen's work is online and in print. https://kazzel.wordpress.com

Kynan Wright aspires to bring the joy he gets from reading to others, and considers himself to be the latest Work in Progress. www.kynanwright.com

Lee Simpson writes short romance and thrillers in simple language so adults can enjoy reading without a dictionary. https://www.instagram.com/

Lincoln Jaques is a Tāmaki Makaurau (Auckland) based writer. His poetry, fiction, travel essays and book reviews have appeared in magazines and collections internationally. He was shortlisted for the 2023 inaugural "At the Bay" hybrid manuscript awards, and was the Runner-Up in the 2022 International Writers' Workshop Kathleen Grattan Prize for a Sequence of Poems (judged by Janet Charman).

Marguerite Laing was born in Auckland, the great-granddaughter of one of New Zealand's most esteemed artists, Charles Blomfield. Many of Marguerite's original works are held in private collections in London, Rome, California, Colorado, Singapore, Tokyo, Sydney, and Auckland. The University of Glasgow's Special Collections Department holds 35 of her originals. https://www.MargueriteLaingArtist.com.

Maris O'Rourke. Maris describes herself as a poet and peregrina, a writer and walker. Writing in various genres and published in a wide range of journals, featured in 20 plus anthologies she has had 10 books published - six children's (two in Te Reo), a family history, a memoir, and two poetry collections.

Marley Ford is an ecologist who uses plants to understand the world around him. Based in Whangārei, he studies a PhD part time while working as a consultant. He enjoys writing scientific articles and science communication pieces with a focus on threatened plants.

Matthew Chamberlain is an emerging New Zealand author delving headfirst into the wide world of speculative fiction. He loves to tell tales about anything he can think of, and stuff he probably shouldn't dwell on too much. He is currently writing novels about strange people with weird problems and spooky pets.

Mayur Wadhwani is a fledgling writer, playwright and game developer. When he is not staring in confusion at his screen, he likes to read, take photographs and enjoy movies.

Melissa Gunn is a scientist and creative who grew up in Tāmaki Makaurau. She enjoys including science in her fiction and is passionate about conservation. She writes, paints, and takes far too many photographs. She also holds a PhD in biology, which she currently uses to add to her story-telling. Her website is www.melissagunn.com

Mitchell Thorburn. Mitch has been exploring and filming in and around the Hauraki Gulf since 2013. Through his studies of Communications, PR, Film, Screen Writing and becoming a Dive Master, he has developed a vision that lead him on a path to tell a story, not just his story but stories of others who contribute to conservation efforts in and around Tīkapa Moana.

Mt Albert Rangers Ashley Lindsay and Sue Glamuzina had a poetry, short story and art session at Mt Albert Rangers where we received some amazing work by their students and leaders.

Patricia Gilmour - as a child she wanted to be both an artist and writer. These aspirations, though, were not pursued until later in her adult life. She joined the local art society and has participated in art exhibitions, joined writing groups, submitted to anthologies and authored her own books.

Paul Barner spends his time writing on things that seem unimportant at first and give them life.

Piers Davies is a long time poet widely published in journals and anthologies in Aotearoa/New Zealand and overseas. He is co-facilitator of Titirangi Poets and co-editor of Titirangi Poets anthologies and Ezines. He has also written feature films 'Homesdale', 'The Cars That Ate Paris' and 'Skin Deep'.

Rina Patel resides in Auckland, is a second generation Indian-New Zealander (Gujarati). Her debut book of poems '22' was published in 2018 and she is fast working on a new set. IG: @snakey.p

S A Thomas is an artist who uses words and colour to try and stitch her heart whole.

Sarah Valentine is a mother, science teacher and writer. When those mythological moments of free-time find her, she loves to be outdoors with her whānau. You can follow her journey on instagram @writing_for_the_joy_of_it

Sandi Hall. Sandi's first novel, The Godmothers, published by The Women's Press (UK, 1982), was followed by a sci-fantasy tale, Wings of Hera, winning an American Librarian's Award. Her short stories have been published in Penguin and New Woman's Press anthologies. Her poems have won poetry slams, one being included in Otago University's 2017 Manifesto

Shan Iyer is an aspiring novelist from India, currently resisting in West Auckland. He holds a BA in creative writing from AUT. In his spare time he drafts Dystopian Science Fiction, Looms Arabian Science Fiction and prototypes his social media platform, Prose weaver.

Shaun Lee is a designer, illustrator, and photographer advocating for the Hauraki Gulf and a citizen scientist studying kekeno mortality.

Sue Carpenter writes (and illustrates) picture books full of New Zealand imagination, and simple language which are dyslexic friendly, for juniors and young adults. She believe everyone should fall into books regardless of their reading abilities.

linktr.ee/susieleenz

Sue Russell is a mixed media artist and jeweller. Her works explore the layers and moods of nature. How there are hidden depths we do not see and how that is also true of people. Suz's pieces are built up in layers adding depth, texture, and interest to the overall piece.

https://www.reconnectnz.co.nz/collections/

Susan Glamuzina is a Kiwi author, artist and poet who feels at home when there's sand between her toes and her thoughts are in the clouds. Sue's been published in A Fine Line, Good Company Lit, Spillwords, Tales of the Domain, Tales from Dominion Road amongst others. Sue was runner up Poetry at the Beach 2022, and won sci and runner up Kids Lit for IWW 2023. She thrives on supporting artists on their publishing journey.

Suzanne Weld. Born and raised in Ōtautahi Christchurch, Suzanne now lives in Tāmaki Makaurau Auckland. She works full-time and is an avid gardener and traveller. She has recently had short pieces of fiction and creative non-fiction published in three anthologies, including in *Tales from Dominion Road.*

Tineke Joustra. Born and raised in the Netherlands, Tineke Joustra moved to New Zealand in 2003, driven by a passion for conservation. Tineke currently holds the position of Operations Manager at Save the Kiwi, and is pursuing her PhD on leopard seals through the University of Canterbury.

Tremaine Ake is a writer of Space Opera and the occasional venture out of Space. He is passionate about mental health, Māori affairs and the Treaty of Waitangi and the steep decline of the environment in New Zealand.

Acknowledgements

Many people are needed to make an anthology possible. This anthology wouldn't have been completed without the help and support of a number of people. We'd like to thank the Auckland Writers Anthology Committee for their tireless hours of hard work compiling, editing, and proofreading this manuscript—in no particular order, thank you to Sue Glamuzina, Kynan Wright, Angela Campbell and Suzanne Weld. Thanks to Melissa Gunn for cover design, proofreading and interior formatting.

To Jade Du Preez, thank you for the anthology logo design and for IT support; to Ashley Lindsay and the Mt Albert Rangers, thank you for your unique contribution to this anthology.

To Kick Arts Radio, and the Dear Writer Podcast, thank you for helping to spread the word of our project. It is so important to have a range of mediums which are open to sharing the breadth of talent and amazing work coming from the creative community.

Thank you to RWNZ, IWW, NZSA, Poetry Live and Anita Arlov for letting your members know about the opportunity to submit work to this anthology; this helped to attract some fascinating submissions.

Finally, thanks to all the writers and artists who submitted poems, short fiction, non-fiction and art to this anthology—it would not have been possible without you. Your pieces, astonishingly diverse and interesting, show your passion for the Hauraki Gulf, Tīkapa Moana.

Other works by Auckland Writers

Find all our anthologies here:
https://www.amazon.com/dp/B0DKLFGH5K

Tales from Dominion Road
Tales of the Domain

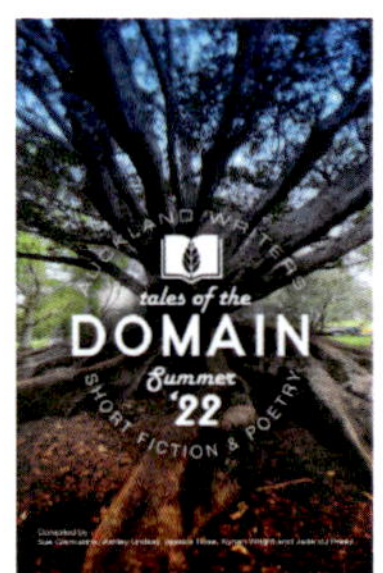

Tales of the Domain

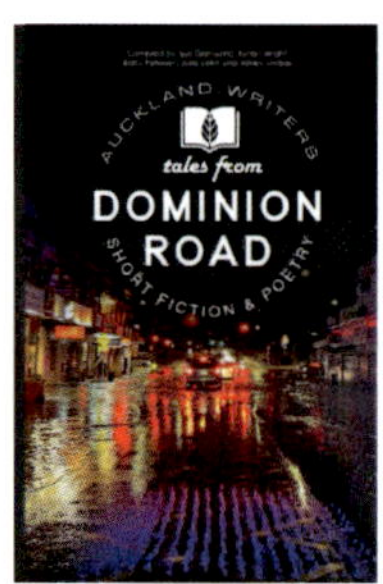

Tales from Dominion Road

About Auckland Writers

Auckland Writers is an online community that is open to writers of any experience level. We provide a space to share resources, inspiration, tips and advice. We also organise workshops and writing critique groups that are available locally and online.

Any profits from this book will support future publications, enabling more writers to see their work in print.

Facebook.com/groups/auck.writers

Facebook.com/groups/618294412686644

Instagram.com/aucklandwritersanthology/

Auckland.writers@gmail.com